W9-BSA-441

A TWO-SPORT SUPERSTAR!

No athlete before him has performed in two major sports with the same degree of success as Bo Jackson. Now you can read about

- His days as a high-school star in baseball, football, and track
- His All-American and Heisman Trophy–winning days at Auburn University
- His tape-measure home runs for the Kansas City Royals
- *And* his long touchdown runs with the Los Angeles Raiders

His skill as an athlete combined with his commitment to his family and teammates make Bo Jackson a total superstar!

Books by Bill Gutman

Sports Illustrated/BASEBALL'S RECORD BREAKERS
Sports Illustrated/GREAT MOMENTS IN BASEBALL
Sports Illustrated/GREAT MOMENTS IN PRO
  FOOTBALL
Sports Illustrated/PRO FOOTBALL'S RECORD
  BREAKERS
Sports Illustrated/STRANGE AND AMAZING
  BASEBALL STORIES
Sports Illustrated/STRANGE AND AMAZING
  FOOTBALL STORIES
BASEBALL'S HOT NEW STARS
BO JACKSON
GREAT SPORTS UPSETS
PRO SPORTS CHAMPIONS
STRANGE AND AMAZING WRESTLING STORIES

Available from ARCHWAY Paperbacks

Most Archway Paperbacks are available at special quantity discounts for bulk purchases for sales promotions, premiums or fund raising. Special books or book excerpts can also be created to fit specific needs.

For details write the office of the Vice President of Special Markets, Pocket Books, 1230 Avenue of the Americas, New York, New York 10020.

BO JACKSON
A BIOGRAPHY

BILL GUTMAN

AN ARCHWAY PAPERBACK
Published by POCKET BOOKS
New York   London   Toronto   Sydney   Tokyo   Singapore

AN ARCHWAY PAPERBACK *Original*

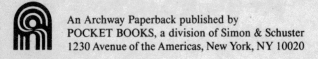

An Archway Paperback published by
POCKET BOOKS, a division of Simon & Schuster
1230 Avenue of the Americas, New York, NY 10020

Copyright © 1991 by Bill Gutman

All rights reserved, including the right to reproduce
this book or portions thereof in any form whatsoever.
For information address Pocket Books, 1230 Avenue
of the Americas, New York, NY 10020

ISBN: 0-671-73363-X

First Archway Paperback printing March 1991

10 9 8 7 6 5 4 3 2 1

AN ARCHWAY PAPERBACK and colophon are
registered trademarks of Simon & Schuster.

Cover photos courtesy of Focus on Sports

Printed in the U.S.A.

IL 5+

To my stepson and pal,
Allen Strang, Jr.

The author would like to thank the following people for their cooperation in supplying background material and information that helped make this book possible:

David Housel, the Sports Information Director at Auburn University and his fine staff; the public relations department of the National Football League, which has been generously helping me with various projects for nearly two decades; and also the media relations departments of the Los Angeles Raiders and the Kansas City Royals.

A special thanks to McAdory High School coaches Dick Atchison and Terry Brasseale, as well as Auburn University head trainer Herb Waldrop, for taking time to share their many recollections and feelings about Bo Jackson.

PART

ONE

Believe it or not, there is a sport that Bo Jackson doesn't like. Even when he was starring in baseball, football, and track as a high schooler and honing his skills for future greatness, Bo rarely stepped onto the basketball court. He played the game only in gym class, when he had no choice. But he still managed to impress his high school coach, Terry Brasseale, with his propensity for doing the unexpected.

Brasseale was Bo's gym teacher one day when the class had to play basketball. As usual, young Bo wasn't hiding his feelings.

"Bo hated basketball," said Brasseale. "He just didn't like it. You knew it every time we played. Well, this one day we finished up when the bell rang and everyone started leaving. I was by the door watching Bo. He picked up one of the basketballs and looked around. All the other boys had gone, and he couldn't see me from where he was standing.

"He put his books down and walked slowly over to the hoop. I watched him standing flat-footed under the basket. Suddenly he just jumped straight up and dunked the ball, two hands over his head. Then he calmly picked up his books and walked out."

Brasseale would have been more astounded by what he had just seen if he hadn't known and coached Bo Jackson. But the coach, like everyone else at McAdory High School in McCalla, Alabama, had already learned that Bo was no ordinary athlete. He was capable of doing the unexpected and the spectacular at any time. It was that way then, and it's still that way now.

Only now the entire country knows about Bo Jackson. They know about his tape-measure home runs with the Kansas City Royals and his long touchdown runs with the Los Angeles Raiders. Before that they knew him from Auburn University where, as a senior, he was given the Heisman Trophy as the best college football player in the land. And they know him from his television commercials that play on his tremendous versatility and success as an athlete.

So while Bo might hate basketball, that doesn't necessarily mean he wouldn't excel at it if he put his mind to mastering the sport. In fact, Bo's achievements in playing and excelling in two major professional sports at the same time have already marked him as one of the most talented and unique athletes in years.

"I don't think there's any question that Bo is the athlete of our time," said his L.A. Raider teammate, All-Pro defensive tackle Howie Long. "This guy has a lot more speed than anybody. He's the guy of our generation. And the great thing about him is that Bo doesn't care about any of it. That's refreshing. He just does what he wants to do. It has nothing to do with the accolades."

The words of Howie Long confirm one thing—the obvious one: Bo Jackson is a very great athlete. But everyone already knows that. However, there is also a hint of something else, something the average sports fan might not have realized. Vincent Edward "Bo" Jackson is also an unusual and unique man.

For years now Bo has faced and made very complex and unusual decisions regarding his life and athletic career. He has said repeatedly that money is not his primary consideration. Today his earning power as an athlete and commercial spokesman is unlimited, yet it seems that he was being sincere when he said it wasn't the dollar that drove him.

He has also maintained that awards, prizes, honors, and records don't mean a whole lot to him. Playing the game for his team and doing it his way are more important to him. Sound corny? Maybe. But, again, it seems he is being candid. As Howie Long said, he's not in it for accolades.

Another of Bo's high school coaches, Dick Atchison, echoed those thoughts when he said this about the man he has known for more than a decade: "I think Bo's playing for the right reasons where a lot of [today's athletes] aren't. Bo's having fun playing. It's not a job to him. I think if it got to be a job, eight hours a day and 12 months a year, he wouldn't do it. There are too many other things he likes to do."

There are some who feel this somewhat refreshing and uncommon attitude might hurt Bo. Because he is playing both major league baseball and professional football with very little time off, they feel he might be

Called "the athlete of our time" by L.A. Raider teammate Howie Long, Bo Jackson has always displayed the intensity and mental toughness needed to play two major sports with little rest in between. The look in his eyes is what tells the story here, as he lugs the ball for the Raiders.
(Courtesy Los Angeles Raiders)

keeping himself from achieving sustained greatness in either sport. But then, too, Dick Atchison may be right. Fun and self-fulfillment may be more important to Bo than immortality in Cooperstown, New York, home of the Baseball Hall of Fame, or Canton, Ohio, where the Pro Football Hall of Fame is located.

Yet some of the things he has accomplished in both sports make him sound like Superman. He can belt tape-measure home runs one month and run 90 yards for a touchdown the next. And he says the whole thing is basically no sweat.

"The athletic part of both sports comes easily for me," Bo has said on more than one occasion. "If I can handle it in my mind, everything else comes easily. Once I leave the ballpark, I go home with a clear mind. I leave everything related to sports at the park. And when I hit the driveway, I become a husband and father."

Again, the too-good-to-be-true picture is an accurate one. Bo has always been a devoted husband and father, a man who loves communicating and working with kids. Despite an always crowded and hectic schedule, he was back at Auburn in 1989, working to complete his degree in family and child development. So when he says his dream is to build a combination day-care center, youth center, and retirement home complex, again you have to believe him.

Unlike many other superstar athletes who seem to crave the limelight, the highly visible Jackson almost shuns it. He has always called himself a private person, and several friends have confirmed that he hates publicity and celebrity. There are times when he prefers to remain in his hotel room on the road rather than venture out. Too many people recognize him and refuse to leave him alone.

Early in 1989 Bo was in downtown Kansas City when he came upon an auto accident. Several drivers had already passed the scene when Bo arrived. He stopped his car, called for an ambulance, then stayed with the injured couple until help arrived. Once they were in good hands, he left the scene before they could even thank him.

A police officer at the scene told the couple, who were from Nashville, Tennessee, that the Good Samaritan was none other than Bo Jackson, the famous athlete.

"I thought he was just a nice guy," the man said. "He was a real gentleman."

Asked about the incident later, Bo shrugged it off as if it were just a part of everyday life.

"There were eight or nine people who slowed down, but went right past them," he said. "I couldn't believe it. Even if it was my worst enemy, I'd stop and help."

It wasn't the first time Bo had done something like that. When he was at Auburn, he once came upon a smoking auto that had hit a guardrail on an interstate. Again Bo stopped, and this time he pulled an injured woman from a vehicle that could have exploded. Once more he left the scene quickly and never told anyone about it, including his wife.

"It wasn't important," he said, later, when his role in the incident was discovered. "It was just the right thing to do."

Bo exhibits a quiet confidence. He doesn't find it necessary to trumpet his own accomplishments. As old friend Terry Brasseale said, "I've never heard him brag, never heard him get cocky."

Yet his confidence and awesome physical power can create an intimidating presence. There was an incident outside a ballpark in 1988 when the Kansas City Royals were on the road. Outfielder Willie Wilson and his wife suddenly found themselves the target of some nasty racial insults as they left the park. Several of the Royals saw what was happening and quickly jumped off the team bus to come to Wilson's aid. For a second it looked as if a brawl would start.

"Everybody on both sides was ready to go," Wilson recalled. "But then they [the hecklers] caught a glimpse of Bo. They quickly left.

"Bo's that kind of person. He doesn't like to be the center of attention, but when it comes down to helping people, he's softhearted. People don't realize what a good person he is, but he's one of the finest persons I've ever known."

The hecklers obviously didn't think of Bo as softhearted. That wasn't why they left. Anyone who has seen the powerful 6'1", 225-pounder play ball would know the reason why. Bo has the classic combination of power and speed that often leads to athletic greatness. And it's all inside a very complex man who hates the limelight but has been squarely in it ever since he first stepped onto the gridiron at Auburn in the autumn of 1982. Since then the Bo Jackson legend has grown to Bunyanesque size. His commercial ventures have served only to enhance his reputation as perhaps the finest all-around athlete in America. As the commercials say, "Bo knows!"

Bo Jackson was born in the small town of Bessemer, Alabama, located just southwest of Birmingham, on November 30, 1962. He was the eighth of 10 children and was essentially raised by his mother, Florence Bond. His early life wasn't always easy. His older brothers were often in trouble, and young Bo was a pretty active, sometimes wild kid.

"I couldn't sit still as a child," Bo has said. "I used to go across a mountain to swim in this old pit. I would sometimes just go out running in the woods. I'd run to the city dump to find old bicycle tires and other things I could use. In fact, I guess I spent a lot of time running back then."

There are two variations on the story of how young Vincent became "Bo." It happened when he was about eight years old. In one version, someone in his family said he was as wild as a boar hog. In the other, he was told he was as mean as a boar hog. Either way, the nickname stemmed from the boar hog. It was later shortened to "bo' hog" and then plain Bo. Both versions seem valid, since he was pretty wild as a kid and, for a time, a little mean.

"There was a time when I'd beat up on kids and take their lunch money," Bo has said. "I wasn't always a good kid, and for a time nobody in my family thought I would turn out all right. But all of a sudden I turned my life around because I didn't want to look at life from the other side of prison bars. The Lord helped me find the straight road."

Bo has said he was about 13 years old when the Lord came into his life. For a time after that he thought about becoming a Baptist preacher. But the lure of sports called to him as well, and the athletic field proved a perfect outlet for his restlessness and need to stay active all the time. Because he loved to run, track was a natural for him. That was his first sport, but soon he was also playing baseball and

Bo's childhood wasn't always easy. He admits to having been wild and sometimes a little mean. As a father, he's considerate and gentle. Here he helps his one-year-old son, Nicholas, go from third to home during a Royals father-kids game in 1989.
(AP/Wide World Photo)

football with his friends. Football did become a bone of contention between Bo and his mother, however. She was afraid he would get hurt and didn't want him to play.

"His mother felt so strongly about Bo not playing football that she even locked him out of the house a few times when he came home from practice," Terry Brasseale recalled. "I remember Bo telling me he had to sleep in the car in front of the house. In fact, his mother never came to see him play a single football game right through his high school days."

Football didn't really start for Bo until about the ninth grade. He played a lot of line on his junior high school team, but didn't really distinguish himself. That was when Dick Atchison met him for the first time.

"No, Bo didn't really do a whole lot in football as a ninth grader," he said. "He only weighed about 165 pounds and was just starting to really develop. That spring, however, he came out for track, and we moved him right up to the varsity so he could compete with the high school boys. Even then, Bo could do many things in track. He was a sprinter, did the high jump, long jump, and triple jump."

When he arrived at McAdory High in nearby McCalla, Alabama, he was just starting to blossom as a football player. He quickly became a starter, swinging back and forth between offense and defense. Though he was already a good player, he still wasn't the superstar performer who would emerge over the next several years. He was closer to a star in track, which was by far his best sport. In both baseball and football he was still raw. But Bo was getting bigger, stronger, and faster—and in a hurry.

Terry Brasseale came to McAdory when Bo was a junior. He recalls visiting the school that summer and seeing Bo Jackson for the first time.

"My first day on campus Bo was working in a program where he helped run the school in the summer," Brasseale said. "He came walking up with his shirt off, and I thought, Lord, I done died and gone to heaven."

While the two coaches began working with the talented youngster, they found it wasn't always easy. Bo was something of a loner, a private person who didn't say much. He was also intelligent and strong-willed, with a propensity to do things his way. For one thing, Bo disliked lifting weights, something all football players do as routinely as lifting a toothbrush.

"Bo hated the weights," Terry Brasseale recalled. "We made him lift, but he hated every minute of it. We'd have to stand there and count sets and reps, or he never would have done it."

It wasn't always easy to communicate with Bo in high school. He had a very bad stutter, which might have been one reason he was quiet. Dick Atchison said that in junior high and early high school Bo couldn't speak a sentence without stuttering badly.

"He got a little better as he got older, and then at Auburn they got him some help and he really improved," Atchison said.

Terry Brasseale recalls hearing Bo being interviewed after he went to Auburn and something struck him as strange.

"Bo kept referring to himself in the third person," Brasseale said. "Instead of saying, 'I want to do this or I hope to do that,' he would say 'Bo wants to do this and Bo hopes to do that.' Well, at first I thought he was starting to sound real cocky. But they had learned at Auburn that the word *I* was triggering the stutter. So he was told to always use his name instead of *I* when he spoke."

It was athletics that began to give young Bo the self-confidence he needed to overcome his stutter and put his troubled youth behind him. But Coach Brasseale says he still had something of a chip on his shoulder right through his junior year.

"He wasn't always the nicest guy in the world," Brasseale said. "He was a loner and seemed to have that chip. I remember about three games into the football season his senior year he just changed. Almost overnight he started being real open and real friendly to his teachers and everyone. And I don't really know what caused it."

Maybe athletic success. For by his senior year Bo Jackson was the talk of the town and far beyond. He had grown to about 218 pounds and had become even faster as he got bigger. Suddenly McAdory High had a force on the gridiron, the track, and the baseball diamond. The small town of McCalla was attracting a different kind of visitor—baseball scouts and college recruiters, all there to watch and speak with Vincent Edward Jackson.

The McAdory football team had been 8–2 and 9–1 during Bo's sophomore and junior years. In 1981, when he was a senior, they were tough again with Bo still the big star. He played tailback, fullback, and defensive end. In addition to that, he was the team's punter and placekicker, and he also returned kickoffs and punts. In other words, he almost never left the field.

"Bo's kickoffs almost always went through the end

zone," said Coach Atchison. "And he won several games for us by kicking field goals. I can't remember his longest, but it was something over 40 yards. He was one heck of a kicker."

Because Bo never left the field, he wasn't always a workhorse runner out of the backfield. He only carried some 12 to 15 times a game, unlike the player he would often be compared with, Georgia star Herschel Walker. According to Dick Atchison, Walker played mostly offense and carried up to 35 times a game. So his running stats were always more impressive than Bo's.

But there was little doubt about Bo's all-around ability. Terry Brasseale described Bo's running style as "wide."

"Bo has huge calves," Brasseale said, "and he always ran wide, with his legs spread out. That gave him even more power, and if defenders didn't lock up, he would run right through them."

There are all kinds of Bo stories from his senior year. In a game against Brookwood, Bo was at defensive end, and the opposing quarterback had dropped back to throw a screen pass. Dick Atchison picks up the story.

"Bo hit the quarterback just as he was letting go of the ball, and both of them hit the ground," Atchison said. "But the quarterback got the ball off to his halfback in the screen area. Bo was like lightning. He jumped off the quarterback, ran down the receiver, and stopped him after only a two-yard gain. He was that quick."

Though Bo did something amazing during each game, his performance in a playoff contest at Legion Field in Birmingham sticks out in Dick Atchison's mind. Legion Field is the stadium where Auburn and Alabama play each year, so it had to be a thrill for high school kids just to perform there. Coach Atchison remembers how Bo showed off another aspect of his all-around game.

"A lot of people didn't realize what a great blocker Bo was, even then," he said. "We had a little halfback named Edwin Mack who was a good friend of Bo's. And on one play we gave the ball to Mack with Bo out in front blocking. Well, he literally blocked four defenders right down to the ground and sprung Edwin Mack for a 65-yard touchdown run. And a year or two later he told a reporter that his favorite play in high school was knocking down those four guys so his buddy could run for a touchdown."

McAdory was 10–1 Bo's senior year, and the star running back gained 1,173 yards on 108 carries for an amazing 10.9 yard-per-carry average. He also scored 17 touchdowns. His size, strength, and speed had the recruiters drooling, and faced with perhaps the first big decision of his life, Bo made it quickly and decisively. Nothing could change his mind.

"Bo never visited but one campus, and that was Auburn," said Terry Brasseale. "He went down there for a visit and got real close to a couple of their players from the Birmingham area, and that was it. He never went to see another school. I remember wanting him to go out to Nebraska. They did a great job recruiting him, but he wouldn't go. Tennessee wanted him, and so did Alabama, but he just kind of closed the door."

There were stories that he didn't like some of the players he had met from Alabama, and he was told by an assistant football coach that if he became a member of the Crimson Tide he shouldn't expect to start until his junior year. Alabama recruiters also supposedly told him that if he went to Auburn he would never taste a victory over Alabama in four years. At that time no one knew not to tell Bo Jackson how something was going to be or that he couldn't do something. If a challenge is offered to him, Bo Jackson takes it.

Once his senior football season was over, Bo concentrated on indoor track, where he won four events at the indoor championships, setting three records along the way. And when spring came, Bo had to divide his time between outdoor track and baseball. But he always made it clear which sport was his favorite.

"Bo would ask me many times while he was in high school if there was any way he could make a good living in track," said Dick Atchison. "If there was, he said he would stay with it. But there was no ironclad guarantee of a stable living from track, and I guess he finally realized it. But he loved the sport, he really did."

Loved it and excelled at it. According to conference rules, he could be entered in only five events at each meet, but Atchison said he was good enough to go in 15. As it was, he was a two-time state decathlon champion, and that competition consisted of ten events. Bo was so adept at the decathlon that he finished tenth in the state as a ninth grader and second as a sophomore before winning it his final two years.

"And the thing is, we didn't even have a track," said Coach Atchison. "We used folding chairs as hurdles and did the best we could. But Bo was always a quick learner. We had no pole vault facilities, either, and Bo would always have to borrow a pole for the decathlon.

He would simply watch some of the other guys vault and copy their technique. And he did it in a short time, and with very little practice."

Like many multi-sport high school stars, Bo had to juggle his time in the spring. Track meets and baseball games were often scheduled at the same time, and that meant setting priorities. But the two coaches, Atchison and Brasseale, worked together and found the right formula.

"Terry and I never put it to Bo in a way that would make him choose one or the other," Dick Atchison said. "We kind of left it up to him. If there was a dual or three-way track meet on the same day as a big baseball game, then he'd go play baseball. And if there was a regular baseball game on the same day as a big track meet with a lot of competition, then he would go to the track meet and miss the baseball game."

In the outdoor track championships, Bo high-jumped six feet eight inches and won the 100-yard dash in 9.5 seconds. As good as he was, however, it was as a baseball player that he began once again to attract attention. For the big kid, who was considered a future All-American football player, was hitting home runs at an unheard-of pace. Even so, he didn't always make things easy for his coach, Terry Brasseale.

"In high school your best athlete usually plays short because that's where the most balls are hit," said the coach. "Bo was really a center fielder, but I put him at short because I needed him there. Yet the position he always wanted to try was catching, but I never used him there. Then there was the pitching problem.

"Bo hated to pitch, but he was just about the best on

the team. In fact, I believe he had a 9–1 record his senior year. He said he would help the team any other way, but not as a pitcher. One day I had him out there, and he walked three straight guys by throwing everything high. He wanted me to take him out. But I didn't move and he walked a couple more, forcing in a pair of runs. All high pitches. And when I still didn't move, he then struck out the side.

"You could always tell when he hated something. He'd be looking around everywhere but not at you, like a little kid. But ultimately, whatever you told him to do, he'd do it. And he only had to hear it once."

Once the home runs started flying out, the scouts came flocking in. And if nothing else, they made life around McAdory High interesting.

"There were games when there were 10 or 12 scouts watching," said Dick Atchison. "And while I hate to say it, the baseball scouts were a lot more ruthless than the college football recruiters. They kept pressuring Bo all year long. He couldn't even go to a track meet without the baseball scouts being there. I remember two scouts from the Montreal Expos following him everywhere during the decathlon championships until I finally had to tell them to leave him alone."

Both coaches still say that Bo constantly amazed them with his athletic feats, a comment that is repeated today by his pro coaches and teammates. In one game during his senior year he hit a high pop behind third. While the left fielder came running in to catch it, Bo took off around the bases at full speed. Because the ball was hit so high, the outfielder misplayed it, and it landed right in front of him. He picked it up and started to throw—but stopped. Bo was already halfway between third and home, completing an inside-the-park home run on a ball that had landed in front of the left fielder.

The pro scouts badgered Coach Brasseale to put Bo in the outfield so they could see his throwing arm. The coach wouldn't give in, but there were throws Bo made from short that showcased his arm anyway.

"One day there was a ball hit deep in the hole," his coach said. "Bo backhanded it on one knee. At this point, most kids would get up, hop, step, and throw. But he just pivoted on his knee and threw a BB to first, all the way across the diamond. He had unreal arm strength and arm speed."

Because Terry Brasseale saw Bo do so many amazing things, he couldn't help bragging about him. Brasseale knew a Kansas City scout named Ken Gonzales from his college days and during Bo's junior year had an occasion to talk with Gonzales.

"I told him I had one kid who was definitely a prospect," recalled Brasseale, "a kid who does things I never saw before. And Ken kind of laughed. He said, 'Well, you might think he's a prospect, but I never heard of him and we usually hear about the top kids. We always get calls about kids who everyone thinks are great, and they're nothing.'

"But because he knew me, Ken came out anyway, and once he watched Bo run and throw, he admitted that Bo would be a number one prospect as a senior."

So the scouts kept coming. And they ultimately saw Bo Jackson set a new national high school record by belting 20 home runs in just 25 games. He hit well over .500 and did it while missing about seven games in favor of track meets. Then, when the season ended, Bo had another decision to make. He had already informed the big league scouts that he was committed to attending Auburn, but that didn't stop the New York Yankees from making him their number two draft choice in the June 1982 free agent draft.

Most young kids would have been easily swayed by the Yanks. After all, the Bronx Bombers were widely considered the greatest, most prestigious franchise in all of sports. They had been in the World Series just the year before and had won it all in 1977 and 1978. So at that time the team was considered a winner. For a kid who had been poor all his life, the Yankee offer of a six-figure contract with a signing bonus in the $150,000 range had to be tempting.

But Bo said no. As would be his pattern in all future decisions, money was not his number-one consideration. Despite his youth, he looked at the decision in a very mature way.

"The money I turned down with the Yankees could only last so long," he said. "But the education I hope to get at Auburn will last a lifetime."

Bo knew there were no guarantees in sports. Even though he had a great deal of self-confidence, he couldn't be sure at that point that he was good enough to be a big leaguer. If he continued to improve in both sports, he'd have time enough to consider future offers for even bigger bucks. So he pretty much had things together, even then.

"By that time you didn't talk to Bo like a kid," Terry Brasseale said. "You talked to him like a man. And you had to be real careful how you put things, because he was smart enough to see right through you. He didn't like the phony rah-rah stuff, and he never got excited."

But Coach Brasseale also knew that Bo was a fierce

Making tough decisions has always been a part of Bo's athletic life. He has learned to become a good listener, weigh his options, and make a thoughtful choice. He was caught in a pensive mood during a 1986 visit to Toronto when he was trying to decide between baseball and football.
(AP/Wide World Photo)

competitor. He recalled one baseball game when the team lost, and his first impression was that Bo didn't care.

"I really let him have it," the coach said. "Chewed him out real good. And he kept looking away like he didn't care. So I told him if he didn't like it to get off the field. But suddenly he looked at me and said, 'Coach, I don't think these guys care about losing.' Then he started to cry, and it really changed my attitude about him. I realized then just how much he hated to lose."

There was an incident at McAdory during Bo's senior year that showed how much he had matured. It happened late in the football season. There was a big pep rally that featured the Who's Who Award, the school's top honor for an athlete. Many expected Bo to win, but the prize was given to another multi-sport star at McAdory who happened to be white.

Tension between blacks and whites grew quickly. Most of the black students wouldn't acknowledge the winner or even applaud. And suddenly the blacks were on one side of the gym, the whites on the other. The rally was quickly disbanded, and the school principal called the seniors into the library for a meeting.

That was when Bo intervened. He asked if he could speak with the students and teachers who had organized the pep rally. Dick Atchison didn't think Bo should become involved, but the youngster said quickly, "I want to get this settled."

"When Bo walked into that room you could hear a pin drop," Dick Atchison said. "He told the group that he didn't come to McAdory to get all the glory and win trophies. 'I came here for my education,' he said, 'and you all better get your act together.' "

Bo's firmness and obvious sincerity quickly defused the situation and made many of the people there realize how silly they were being. It was another example of his maturity. He wasn't involved in sports for money or glory—he was already doing it for his own reasons.

There was something about him that both his high school coaches noticed, something that would influence the choices he'd make in the coming years.

"This may sound crazy," Dick Atchison said, "but both Terry and I noticed in high school that Bo would sometimes get bored to death. He couldn't stay with any one thing for too long."

Coach Brasseale agreed. "He's the type who always has to play a bunch of different sports," he said. "He just gets tired of playing one sport, and by the time the season is ending he's already looking forward to doing something else."

Bo Jackson graduated from McAdory High School in June of 1982. He had earned good grades and would be admitted to Auburn on academic merit as well as for his athletic skills. He left plenty of memories behind in McCalla. Difficult at times? Yes. Strong-willed and sometimes stubborn? Definitely. Tough to coach? He could be. Yet perhaps Terry Brasseale best caught the essence of Bo's high school days when he said, "He is still the greatest thing that happened to me as a high school coach."

PART

TWO

Auburn University was about two hours from Bessemer, and Bo Jackson liked the idea of being close to home. He probably took comfort in the fact that his family and friends weren't far from him. Bo went to Auburn in the autumn of 1982 knowing he had to keep up his grades while going out for three sports. So it wouldn't be easy.

Football, of course, came first. And it didn't take long for head coach Pat Dye and the rest of the Auburn Tiger staff to see they had a player of unlimited potential. Ironically, Bo was not Auburn's top recruit at running back that year. There was another runner who was more highly publicized than Bo, and he was penciled in as the primary back—that is, until they took a good look at Bo.

"This youngster is the biggest guy I've ever coached who can run that fast," said backfield coach Bud

Casey. "If he can handle all of the pressure and everything, he should be able to do about what he wants to out there."

"Every day he goes on the field he does something extraordinary," said head coach Dye. "And hands—I haven't seen him drop a ball yet."

In other words, the feeling was that Bo could do it all. At 6'1", 220 pounds he was a combination Clydesdale and racehorse, and once the preseason scrimmages began, he quickly showed he was even better than people thought.

Bo carried the ball 11 times in the team's first two major scrimmages and gained 172 yards, an average of 15.6 yards per tote. At one point in the second scrimmage he took a handoff and tried to go around the left end. A pair of defenders had him trapped behind the line of scrimmage, but he bounced off both would-be tacklers and turned the play into a nine-yard gain. Later in the same scrimmage he turned a simple dive play over the middle into a 73-yard touchdown run as he left three defenders stretched out on the ground.

Performances like that caused an inevitable comparison to Herschel Walker, who was in the process of rewriting the NCAA rushing record book at the University of Georgia. Walker would be going into his junior year in 1982 and had been a superstar, a workhorse runner, since he was a freshman.

"Herschel used to be my idol when I was in high school," Bo admitted, "but now I don't have time for idols."

It was also pointed out that Bo was wearing the same uniform number as Walker, number 34. Bo's explanation was that he had been number 43 in high school, and because that was already taken at Auburn he simply reversed the numerals and asked for 34. But because he and Walker were about the same size, both had blazing speed, and both wore the same number, the comparisons would continue.

Bo's varsity debut came in the team's opener against Wake Forest. He didn't start, but was in the game before long. He wound up leading all rushers with 123 yards on just 10 carries. And his 43-yard touchdown run early in the fourth quarter helped put the game on ice.

"I don't think the coaches expected me to have as good a game as I did," Bo said. "I didn't expect it, either. But you have to remember that Wake has a small defense and they were trying to contend with a big offense."

Statements like that would become typical for Bo. He always tried to divert the spotlight from himself, make his triumphs seem to be part of a team effort, and not seek the attention of the media. It didn't always work, but he tried. One thing was certain after the Wake Forest game, however. The starting halfback had gained just one yard on one carry before Bo took over. In his second game Bo would be the starter, running out of the halfback spot in the Auburn wishbone.

People were quick to point out that Herschel Walker also became a starter the second game of his freshman year, but there was a difference. Georgia always ran out of the I-formation, which made Walker the tailback, the featured back in that formation. And it wasn't unusual for him to get upwards of 30 carries a game.

Bo would be running out of the wishbone, a more

wide open formation that centered around the quarterback and generally included many rollouts and options. The QB was the hub of the attack, and when he rolled out he could run, throw, or pitch back to another runner. With the wishbone, Bo would probably get only 10 to 12 carries a game. There was no way he would compile huge numbers within the wishbone.

That, basically, was the strategy. Bo quickly solidified his position as the team's top rusher. However, he was doing it despite getting about 12 carries a game. When the coaches decided how the wishbone could best attack a defense, it was with the entire offense in mind, not just Bo.

For example, Bo had a fine game against Tennessee, running for 110 yards as the Tigers won. The next week, however, in a loss to powerful Nebraska, Bo was handed the ball just five times and was never really a factor. It had to be a bit frustrating for a youngster who was willing to run as often as the coaches wanted. He missed nearly two games with a bruised thigh at midseason, but by the time the ball club got ready to play top-rated Georgia, the Tigers were 7–2 and Bo was the leading rusher with 657 yards. In fact, he led the Tigers in six offensive categories.

"He's made a tremendous contribution to the team so far this year," said Coach Dye. "We managed to beat Georgia Tech without him and then played two and a half quarters without him at Mississippi State. But he came in and gave us a big boost in the third and fourth periods."

The other halfback in the wishbone was Lionel James, a 5'7", 165-pound speedster. He would become Bo's closest friend and the team's number two ground gainer. James said that Bo's potential explosiveness often became a decoy since defenses were beginning to key on him.

"We run some misdirected plays where they lean toward Bo and then hand it back to me. That often gives me a half-step advantage and that's all I need."

It was late in the season by this time, and some of the quotes from Bo had a strange, almost hollow ring to them. Maybe Dick Atchison and Terry Brasseale, his coaches back at McAdory, would have recognized the symptoms.

Asked if his accomplishments as a freshman had gone beyond his goals, Bo said, "Right now, I don't have any goals. I just go every Saturday and play. I just go out and play the sport."

Then, asked if he was enjoying his first season as a collegiate star, Bo responded quickly. "I like it," he said, "but right around this time I'm ready to get into track, because I don't have my mind on football like I did the first of the year."

Then, asked what he would think about the season being extended if Auburn received a bowl bid, Bo said, "That's something I'll have to cope with."

Was it boredom? Was the restless Jackson ready for another sport? It certainly sounded that way, and anyone reading the story might have found it a bit odd that this talented freshman wasn't more enthusiastic. What no one realized at the time was that a major crisis in Bo's life was just around the corner.

The Tigers lost to Georgia, with Herschel Walker easily outgaining Bo because he carried the ball so often. Walker, running from the I-formation, had 177 yards. Bo, carrying far less often from the wishbone, had 58. It would be the only time the two great backs would meet on the college gridiron.

Next up was the biggest game of the year against archrival Alabama. It was a game that Auburn had not won in a decade. Then, just a few days before that clash, Bo's friends couldn't find him in his room. In fact, they couldn't find him anywhere on campus. It was a Friday night, and a few of his friends were really concerned. Where was he?

Unknown to everyone, the star running back was sitting at the Greyhound bus station in nearby Opelika, Alabama. Bo had been at the station since 6:00 P.M. and was wrestling with a major decision. Should he get on a bus to Birmingham and go home?

"I was depressed and disillusioned with a lot of things," he said later. "I didn't think I could keep on handling the pressure that had been put on me."

So Bo sat quietly, trying to decide what to do. He watched seven or eight buses leave for Birmingham, and while he came close, he couldn't bring himself to board. But all the time he kept thinking of home.

"I missed everyone," he recalled. "And each time a bus would leave I'd tell myself that I would catch the next one. But I never did."

At two o'clock in the morning Bo was still sitting there wondering what to do. That was when the night supervisor at the station came over to him and said, "Son, you've been hanging around here a long time. Either buy a ticket or leave."

The ultimatum seemed to bring Bo out of it. He knew what he had to do and promptly hitched a ride back to the campus and the athletic dorm. Of course he had broken curfew, and for that he had to be punished. The penalty was "100 stadiums," which meant running up and down the steps of the east stands of Jordan-Hare Stadium 100 times. But Bo gladly did his penance, for once again his mind was clear and he knew what he had to do.

"I thought about all the people back home who were looking forward to seeing me succeed in sports," Bo said. "If I had quit and gone home, then they would think I was no good. And I had never been a quitter in anything I did. I was also used to high school football seasons, which lasted about nine weeks. Suddenly we were in our thirteenth or fourteenth week, and I was just tired of it all."

Back at school, Bo finished preparations for the Alabama game. He remembered Crimson Tide recruiters telling him he wouldn't start at Alabama until he was a junior and that if he went to Auburn he'd never taste victory over the Tide. He took the field with his teammates for what would turn out to be an epic battle.

And if it hadn't been for Bo Jackson, the Tide undoubtedly would have kept their winning streak intact. Not only did he run for 114 yards, but his 53-yard jaunt, his season best, helped to turn the game around. Then, with the Tigers trailing in the fourth quarter, Bo dove over the goal line from three yards out for what would prove to be the winning score. Auburn won the game, 23–22, and for the first time Bo Jackson was a real hero, the toast of the town.

Bo finished the season with 829 yards on 127 carries, good for a 6.5 average and nine touchdowns. He averaged 75.4 yards a game with a long gain of 53 yards. The Tigers didn't throw much, so Bo caught just five passes for 64 yards. Teammate Lionel James gained 779 yards and ran at a 6.9 per-carry clip. The two backs, now close friends, had similar stats out of the wishbone.

Bo's speed and power out of the backfield can even be seen in a publicity photo. Once he put the helmet on, Bo became one of the greatest collegiate running backs ever.
(AP/Wide World Photo)

"If I'd made just two more blocks somewhere along the line, Lionel James would have been Auburn's leading rusher," Bo teased. But by then everyone knew that Bo was going to be the main man. As a freshman, he was named to the Football News Freshman All-American team, was an All-Southeast Conference selection and SEC Freshman of the Year, but he didn't have much time to rest on his laurels. First he had to play in the Tangerine Bowl; then he moved right into his second sport, indoor track.

Once again it didn't take Bo long to make his mark. His debut came in the LSU Invitational Meet at Baton Rouge. In his first preliminary heat, Bo ran the 60-yard dash in 6.18 seconds, the fourth fastest time in Auburn history. Those who did better were all world-class sprinters. In the final of the event Bo ran a 6.20 and was nipped at the tape by Rice's Vince Courville, also considered one of the top sprinters in the country at the time.

But his 6.18 in the prelim was good enough to rank him third in the conference, behind Herschel Walker (that man again), who ran a 6.15, and Alabama's Emmitt King, who had a 6.17 clocking.

"Bo has been practicing every day since coming out," said his coach, Mel Rosen. "He just missed one day when he went over to hit some baseballs, but he came back and ran that evening. He has been working mainly on his starts since he joined us. In high school he used to come out quickly, then stumble before he'd get rolling. He has changed his start a little bit and has developed a smoother running style."

The coach predicted Bo would run around a 6.36 in his first meet. As usual, the former McAdory High star surprised everyone.

"When I saw him blow out of the blocks and get a solid start in his trial heat I knew he would have a great race."

Bo had a successful track season, then had to rush right into baseball. Because indoor track overlapped the baseball season, he got a late start. Bo played in 26 games, getting 19 hits in 68 at-bats for a modest .279 average. Among his hits were four home runs and 13 runs batted in. Though he played a solid center field and showed a great deal of raw talent, it wasn't a super baseball season for him. No All-American honors, no accolades, and the major league teams were not nipping at his heels. But he had become the first three-sport letterman at Auburn in 30 years.

During the off-season Bo returned home and got a job in a bank in Birmingham. It was something he wanted to do. He felt that working with the public daily would help him in his dealings with the media and the public during the upcoming football season.

"I got to meet a lot of nice people," Bo said of the experience. "And I think I learned some things about dealing with people and situations. One of my coworkers was a big Alabama fan, and the first day I came to work she took a swing at me with a big batch of checks. She was just kidding around. It was fun."

Back at Auburn for his sophomore year, Bo knuckled right down to the business of studies and football. The Tigers were looking forward to a big year, and Coach Dye, who had said Bo was already good enough to play in the pros, wanted his rock-solid running back to have a big season. The coach felt there was a change in Bo's outlook right from the start. Number 34 was acting like a leader from the first day of practice.

Another person who saw the emergence of Bo as a leader was the Tigers' head trainer, Herb Waldrop. A trainer for 30 years now, Waldrop says that his relationship with the players is different from that of a head coach. He often ends up more of a friend, and during Bo's tenure at Auburn, the two became very close.

"One of the first things I noticed about Bo was his tremendous sense of humor," Waldrop said. "And he was very pleasant to be around. He was a very mature person, a smart person, knowledgeable in a lot of areas. You could just sit down and talk with him. Bo could discuss anything. We often talked about hunting and fishing, but we talked about a lot of other things, too."

As the 1983 season got set to open, Bo also talked about some of the changes that had occurred in the past year. "Last year I just didn't know how to deal with the entire situation," he said. "I didn't know anybody then, but now knowing so many nice people has made it easier.

"This year I'm trying to be a leader on the field. There were times last year when I was stubborn, even a jackass sometimes. This year I don't want to be the oddball. I don't want to be the guy who louses up practice. This team has high goals. To reach them we've got to pull together, and that includes me."

The Tigers opened the season against Southern Mississippi, and it was Bo's friend Lionel James who had the big game. The team was still running out of the wishbone, and James gained 172 yards on 16 carries. Bo had a strong game as well, with 73 yards on 11 tries. He also grabbed a 44-yard touchdown pass to help key the victory and set the scene for the season. Auburn truly had a fine team, and before long it was apparent that Bo Jackson was its finest player.

The only problem was the wishbone. No matter how you cut the pie, that formation just isn't geared to feature any single back. While the Tigers continued to win, Bo had to be content with a limited number of carries. After five games he had carried only 61 times for 389 yards. That was an average of 12 carries and some 78 yards a game. Still, Bo was averaging nearly 6.5 yards a carry, and projected to 30 carries a game, his stats would have been eye-popping.

Tiger coaches must have realized that. Head coach Pat Dye said Bo was "the best running back in America. Line the others up one at a time and I don't see one being better. Having Bo sitting back there is an awesome sight."

Yet because of his obvious talent there were those who felt Bo should carry more. In the Tigers' lone loss, a 20–7 decision to Texas, Bo got the call a mere seven times. Coach Dye was also concerned about that.

"With the kind of talent and ability Bo has," the coach said, "he could get carried away with what people are telling him. There's no question in our minds that we're making an effort to get the football to him. But Bo understands we are a team-oriented offensive football team."

Bo did understand. Except for the loss to Texas, the team was winning and continued to win. That was the important thing. Running back coach Bud Casey attributed Bo's positive attitude to his maturity.

"Bo grew up since last year," said Casey. "When I see Bo, I see a young man who has developed the physical and mental and spiritual facets of his life. He also has more talent than anybody I've ever been around and does more with it. On top of that, he's a team player. He doesn't pout because he's not getting the ball or because he's having to block."

But Bo's pace did pick up. The night before the Florida game he couldn't sleep because of an upset stomach. But the next afternoon he went out and gave the Gators upset stomachs, gaining 196 yards on 16 carries as the Tigers won again, 28–21. He had touchdown runs of 55 and 80 yards against a defense that hadn't allowed a run of more than 25 yards in four years. It was his greatest day as a collegian, prompting Coach Dye to say, "If he's not an All-American, there ain't one in America!"

Later he picked up 115 yards against a Georgia defense that had been giving up a total of only 106 yards a game. After 10 games Bo had gained 957 yards and was averaging 7.0 yards a carry. There was no denying him now. He was without a doubt one of the best running backs in America. There was even talk about him possibly winning the Heisman Trophy as a sophomore. But typical of Bo, he was always ready to give the credit to others.

"I haven't given it much thought," he said. "If I do win the Heisman—and I doubt that I will—it will be because of my teammates blocking in front of me. It won't be because of anything I do.

"But for me, the Heisman just isn't in the picture. I just work toward improving. I want to be a better person, a better blocker, a better runner. The goal I set every year is to have a better season than I did the year before. That's all."

However, that was quickly becoming enough. In

fact, with the season-ending contest with Alabama coming up, Bo Jackson had saved the best for last. Once again he made the Crimson Tide regret not having recruited him differently, for Bo was all over the field, using his power and speed to the ultimate.

In the opening minute of the second period Bo brought the crowd to its feet with an electrifying 69-yard touchdown run. But the Tide fought back and took a 20–16 lead late in the third period. Then on the first play from scrimmage following the kickoff, Bo broke loose again, using his speed and power to ramble 71 yards for the touchdown that broke Alabama's back. He also helped control the ball in the final period. Auburn took a 23–20 victory.

Bo was once again the toast of the town. He had run for a career-best 256 yards to key the victory and enable the Tigers to turn back the Tide for the second straight year. His performance also certified his being a consensus All-American as a sophomore, Auburn's first sophomore All-American since Walter Gilbert back in 1933.

He did it on the strength of 1,213 yards rushing on just 158 carries, an average of 7.7 yards a pop. He had a long gain of 80 yards, scored 12 touchdowns, caught another 13 passes for 73 yards and two more scores. What's more, he did it averaging just over 14 carries a game. So he still wasn't a heavy-duty runner by a long shot, but everyone now knew how talented and explosive he was. The Alabama game on national television proved that once and for all.

Bo would finish his sophomore season by gaining 138 yards and being named the Most Valuable Player in the Sugar Bowl game on New Year's Day. Leading

Auburn to yet another win on top of winning the Southeastern Conference title was the icing on the cake. The Tigers were the third-ranked team in the country in most postseason polls, and his sensational season put Bo Jackson squarely in the limelight. Now there was no getting away from it for him—he was a superstar and a celebrity.

The first crisis to arise out of Bo's success was a rumor that he was negotiating with the Baltimore Colts of the National Football League for a multimillion-dollar pact that would enable him to leave Auburn after his sophomore year. Bo denied the story immediately.

"Money can't buy happiness," he said, "not even $2.5 million. I realize I'm taking something of a chance because you never know when an injury might occur, but it's just a chance I'm going to take. I'm just not interested in playing pro ball until after my senior year."

Bo also said that he would never lie about his intentions, as other athletes had, saying they would not leave, but then leaving when the dollar signs became big enough.

"Naturally I'm keeping my options open," Bo said. "But if I ever leave, it won't be because of my greed for money."

The NCAA looked into the rumors and found that Bo had not in any way attempted to negotiate with the Colts. The whole thing was brought about when the Colts' owner, Robert Irsay, angry that he couldn't re-sign one of his running backs, told some people he could probably get Bo Jackson instead for $2.5 million.

"We're aware of what has been in the papers," said an NCAA official, "and on the face of what we've seen, we don't plan to pursue an investigation."

Bo, of course, didn't have time to think about the Colts. He wasn't going and that was that. Now it was on to track and to his studies. Playing three sports wasn't easy, especially with the increased demands on his time as a superstar.

"There is a time for classes and a time for athletics and very little time for anything else," he said. "When I'm not in class or practicing, I'm talking to someone. When I'm not doing that, I just try to isolate myself. It makes me feel good that people want my autograph, but mainly when I go places, I zip in and zip out. I don't stay anywhere too long."

Bo did travel home as often as he could. There were no more late-night decisions in deserted bus stations. He went home to enjoy his family and friends; then he returned to Auburn without a qualm.

"I go home to be with my family, mainly my three nephews and one niece," he said. "The first thing I do when I go home is to pick them up. Then we go to McDonald's or somewhere and just spend time together."

Of course as soon as Bo moved on to track, there were again questions about his playing three sports. They were the same questions he'd heard at McAdory and would continue to hear for years to come. But the answer he gave during his sophomore season foreshadowed things to come.

"Sports is a hobby with me," he told a reporter. "It's something I did to keep out of trouble in high school and something I do to stay in shape now. I stay in shape playing football, then track, and then baseball. And I don't think playing all three sports will hurt me."

As for his studies, Bo often retreated to the basement of the study lounge in the Haley Center at Auburn. There he could get away from everyone. As he said, it was just Bo and the books.

"Right now I'm in general curriculum, but I'm thinking about majoring in psychology. I'd like to work with kids. I've been around them all my life and would like to help them avoid some of the mistakes I made."

Despite his schedule, Bo never fell behind in his grades. Because of the demands on his time, he sometimes had to take a lighter course load than he wanted. But he was far from the stereotype of a dumb jock. He was an intelligent, thinking person who didn't let his mind stagnate. In fact, he used the same intelligent approach to athletics.

Head trainer Herb Waldrop called Bo "a very intelligent athlete. He never abused his body, and if there was a problem he would let me know."

Bo did make one concession to his schedule as a sophomore. He decided to give up baseball in the spring of 1984 to concentrate on track. It was the first time since he entered high school that he wouldn't be playing baseball in the spring. And that, of course, made people feel all the more certain that he would pursue football as a professional. He seemed to be putting baseball on the back burner.

Bo had a good track season, though not a great one. There were those who felt Bo didn't work as hard as he could have. He missed spring football because of track, yet even in an Olympic year, he didn't set his goals on qualifying for the NCAA trials. The trials would produce the United States track team for the Summer Olympics at Los Angeles. At one point, however, he was just one-hundredth of a second off the qualifying time in the 100-meter dash.

"I really wasn't into qualifying," Bo said candidly. "There were times when I could have qualified, but even if I had, it would have taken up what summer I had to be home and rest. As a junior and senior in high school one of my goals was to go to the Olympics. But after I came to Auburn and became so involved in football, played a little baseball, and ran a little track, I was ten times as tired as I had ever been before. There is only a certain limit your body can do."

Basically, Bo was saying that he wasn't Superman. Like everyone else, he reached a point where he needed a rest. He just couldn't do it all. It also sounded as if football were now his major sport— baseball and track only something to keep him busy. There would certainly be a great deal of hype before the 1984 football season began. And before it ended, Bo Jackson would find his body and character being tested as never before.

There was pressure almost from the beginning of the season. For one thing, many preseason polls picked the Tigers as the number one team in the country. Also, after Bo's sensational sophomore season, he was widely acknowledged as the best running back—and maybe the best player—in the college ranks. The reward for the best player was the Heisman Trophy. In the minds of many, Bo was the logical front runner even before he made a single block or tackle.

"I'm not thinking about the Heisman or what I've

got to do to win the Heisman," Bo said on more than one occasion, since reporters and media people tended to ask the same question over and over again. "Lately it seems the Heisman is the only thing anyone wants to talk to me about. I will say this much. Every football player wants to win the Heisman Trophy. It's everybody's dream, including mine. But right now the Heisman is just another trophy, something I can't really think about at this point in the season."

Bo also said that if he won the Heisman, the trophy would go to the person most responsible for his success—his mother.

"My mother is very special," he said. "She raised 10 kids, nine in just a three-room house, and she always had food on the table for us. She's worked every day of her life, and I admire her for all the sacrifices she's made. Without her, I wouldn't be at Auburn and I wouldn't be the person I am."

Besides the Heisman, there were always questions about Bo's future, about the possibility of his leaving Auburn for the moneyed pastures of the pro world. Those were also questions that he couldn't avoid.

"Right now I can't say I'll stay [for his senior year], and I can't say I'll go. But no matter what I do, people are going to call me crazy. If I stay, they're going to call me crazy for turning down all that money. If I go, people are going to call me crazy for leaving college. I'll be criticized either way, but I'm willing to take the criticism no matter what I decide."

Bo was also reminded that his illustrious predecessor as college football's premier running back, Herschel Walker, had an insurance policy against injury. Such a policy was perfectly legal under NCAA rules if the player was willing to pay the premiums himself. Bo said he had no such policy.

"The way I see it, if I thought that way I'd have a tendency to worry about getting hurt. Once you start thinking about getting hurt, you'll get hurt. I believe if you go full speed, you're never going to get hurt. It's when you slack up and go half speed that you run the risk of injury."

He also felt he was a smarter runner now than when he was a freshman and predicted any injury he sustained would be minor. That was the only kind of injury he had ever had.

The Tigers were scheduled to open the season against the defending national champion Miami Hurricanes. They would be opening early, since they were invited to play Miami at the New Jersey Meadowlands in the annual Kickoff Classic, the first college football game of the year. The game would be a tough one, for despite its preseason number one ranking, the 1984 Tigers were a much younger club than the 1983 team, which had won its final 10 games in a row.

It turned out to be a real battle. The huge Miami players dominated Auburn at the line of scrimmage, and Bo's offensive line had trouble moving the Hurricane defenders out. Bo got the ball 20 times, a high number of carries from the wishbone, and he gained 96 yards. But for him that was considered mediocre yardage for 20 carries. The Hurricanes, meanwhile, rode home on the strong arm of quarterback Bernie Kosar and won the game, 20–18, in a mild upset.

The Tigers had to face their second game against powerful Texas two weeks later. The Longhorns had pinned the only loss on Auburn the year before, giving them a 20–7 whipping in Bo's least productive game as a collegian. In addition, the loss to Miami wasn't a good way for a young team to start the season.

"I think the Miami game lessened the whole team's confidence," Bo said. "That's what we have been working on for two weeks, trying to rebuild our confidence."

But there was another problem for the Tigers, one that could prove more serious than a little lack of confidence. Bo had sustained a sprained ankle in the Miami game, the kind of minor injury he had talked about before the season. Only it wasn't healing as fast as he had hoped. He missed some practice time the first week, and the Monday of the second week he still wasn't back to normal.

"Right now he's not doing so good," said Coach Dye. "But we're hoping by Saturday he'll be 100 percent."

Hoping wasn't a very confident word. Bo was usually a fast healer, and sure enough, he was in the starting lineup when the Tigers met the Longhorns in Austin, Texas, on September 19. It was a hard-fought, high-scoring game with the outcome still up for grabs in the third quarter. Bo had been grinding it out, but was having some trouble with the big Longhorn defenders. They were keying on him all day. Then he broke one.

It was a typical Jackson run—he outmuscled some defenders and outran others—and it brought the crowd to its feet. Bo seemed to be off to the races, even though he was being chased by Jerry Gray, an All-American defensive back. But nobody caught Bo Jackson when he was in the clear.

Only this time somebody did. Bo favored his sprained ankle, and Gray nailed him with a hard tackle after the big guy had rambled 53 yards, his longest run of the game. When he got up, he didn't look right, but he went back to the huddle. He played several more downs, then came out of the game.

"As soon as I hit the ground," Bo would say later, "I knew I had hurt myself real bad. I didn't tell anyone I was hurt because I wanted to play again."

On the sidelines the coaches had asked if he could still play, and Bo had said yes, but it soon became obvious that he couldn't. His shoulder had been separated.

"I asked Bo if he was hurt, and he said he was," Coach Dye explained. "But he said he could still play. I think that shows what kind of man he is and what kind of competitor he is. We wouldn't have put him back in the game if we had known he had a separation."

A separated shoulder, in this case, meant surgery. When Bo realized the extent of the injury, he wept on the flight back to Auburn. It was his first major injury, and that's never easy for any athlete to take, especially such an active and complete one as Bo. Two days later he went under the knife for the first time in his career. The surgeon said everything went fine, but that Bo would probably be out for the season.

"There were no complications," the surgeon said. "Bo will be in a sling for three or four weeks; then he can start using the arm. But I wouldn't anticipate Bo being able to play again this season."

Bo was quick to point out that the gimpy ankle had helped cause the injury. If the ankle hadn't been hurt, Gray wouldn't have caught him. Also, the turf at Austin Memorial Stadium was rock hard, which didn't help. Bo's earlier statement about little injuries

Inactivity is the toughest thing for Bo Jackson to endure. Just the sight of him on the Auburn bench after the shoulder injury that shortcircuited his junior season confirms that. Bo was so anxious to get back that the ultimate speed of his recovery amazed everyone, including the doctors.
(AP/Wide World Photo)

leading to big injuries proved true. The ankle forced him to go at less than full speed, and that, according to Bo, was when injuries happen.

The question was where to go from here. If he was out for the entire season, he could choose to become a redshirt and have another two full seasons of eligibility left. That meant he could stay at Auburn for a fifth year and play another season of football. Bo didn't want that and he made it quite clear.

"The decision isn't hard," he said. "I don't allow decisions to get hard. I just say yes or no. When the time comes for me to leave Auburn and go on to a pro career, I'll be ready to go. Besides, Coach Dye said he would never dream of keeping me here another two years. So I think the redshirt is out of the question."

That took care of that. But it wasn't long after the surgery that Bo realized something else. He was bored silly. It was the first time in his life that he had been forced to be inactive, and he was finding it hard to take. His daily routine at first consisted of watching soap operas, talking on the phone, studying, and napping. That wasn't Bo Jackson.

"I'll go to sleep," Bo said, "then wake up and look at my watch and find that only 10 minutes passed. I've got nothing but time on my hands."

Soon he realized there was only one answer.

"I'm itching to get back," he said. "I've got nothing else to do."

Suddenly Bo had a goal. He was determined to play again before the season ended. At first he targeted the Alabama game on December 1. But once he threw himself into his rehabilitation program full force, he began moving up the date, talking about being ready for Georgia on November 17. Those who predicted he would be out for the season were skeptical. Not even Bo Jackson could be back on the gridiron that quickly.

Bo threw himself into his rehab program because he didn't like what was happening to him physically right after the surgery.

"I was very depressed," he said. "All I would do was eat fruit and drink water. I went from 228 pounds to 210 within a week."

So he began to work. He got rid of the sling in early October and began exercising with a 10-pound dumbbell. He was constantly working the arm, windmilling it as he walked on campus, trying to get the range of motion back. A week later he was running, and the doctors began to marvel at how quickly he was recovering.

"Bo had a strong combination going for him," said head trainer Herb Waldrop. "He was a very intelligent athlete who knew what he could and couldn't do, and he was extremely loyal to his team. Three weeks after the surgery he was talking about coming back, because he felt he could help the team. Even I was skeptical, so we began to consult with the doctor. Though the healing process was still taking place, Bo had really rehabbed himself as far as strength and motion were concerned. So we began to prepare a special type of shoulder pad for him to wear when he returned."

Six weeks after the surgery that was expected to keep him out all year, Bo was back at practice. It wasn't full contact, but he took some snaps and carried the ball a couple of times. And there was little doubt that being back with his teammates felt good.

"There's still some soreness," he said. "But that's to be expected. I've been working out for a few weeks, but this was the first time I tried to really do something where I exert myself. I'd really like to get back as soon as possible, but only when the doctor gives me the okay. I've missed being with my teammates. It hasn't been a lot of fun."

Ironically, the team had pulled together after Bo's injury and won six straight games going into the Florida contest on November 3. Bo surprised a lot of people by appearing on the sideline in uniform as the game began. Then, with 4:36 remaining in the first period, he found himself in the ball game. He wound up playing 27 minutes, carrying five times, and gaining just 16 yards. Fortunately he came out of the game no worse for wear. The bad news was that the Tigers were beaten decisively, 24–3.

"I'm still not in the best shape," Bo said. "I wasn't worried about contact, just about stamina. I didn't know how long I would be able to stay in there. Things should start getting better in the next week or two."

No one missed the irony of Bo's return. The team had lost its first two games to Miami and Texas, the game in which Bo was hurt. And now they lost to Florida when he returned. So the ball club was 0–3 with Bo in the lineup and 6–0 without him. But he rounded into shape during the next two weeks. In fact, in a win over Cincinnati, Bo scored three touchdowns and gained 59 yards in just one half of action. Finally it was time for the season finale against Alabama. Bo had been the hero of the last two victories over the Tide and looked to the game as a way of coming all the way back from his injury.

As usual, it was a hard-fought game. Bo didn't break any big ones, but there was little doubt that the Tide was keying on him. By late in the fourth period

Alabama held a slim, 17–15, lead, but the Tigers were driving and the stage seemed to be set for Bo to be the hero for the third straight year.

Finally it came to this. The Tigers had a fourth down on the Alabama one-yard line with 3:27 left in the game. A field goal would put them ahead by one, but would also give the Tide a chance to drive far enough to maybe win it with a three-pointer of their own. Coach Dye decided to go for the touchdown. And just about everyone watching expected Bo Jackson to get the football.

Maybe that was why the Tigers decided to run halfback Brent Fullwood on a sweep around the right side. Bo was supposed to lead the play, but somehow there was a mixup. Bo faked into the line on the left side, while quarterback Pat Washington gave the ball to Fullwood, who was running right. The young halfback, who had emerged when Bo was hurt, couldn't get into the end zone. The Tide had held and would win the game, 17–15. And much of the blame fell to Bo, who had gone the wrong way.

"It's just one of those no-win situations," Bo said, afterward. "What if I had run the right way and we still didn't score? Or what if I had gotten the ball and we didn't score? People would still be saying that Coach Dye messed up."

The coach had come under fire for not trying the short field goal. Now both coach and star had to take the blame. Bo had to be upset by the final turn of events. It was bad enough that he had missed so much time because of injury, gaining just 475 yards on 87 carries for the year. But to make a mistake in the Alabama game, well, that was the topper. It depressed

Bo, and for a time he talked about skipping his senior year and following Herschel Walker's lead by signing with the fledgling United States Football League. (The National Football League did not sign underclassmen then.)

He got some of his old fire back when his 61-yard touchdown run in the fourth quarter enabled the Tigers to top Arkansas 21–15 in the postseason Liberty Bowl. Up to that time he had gained just 31 yards on 14 carries, and the whispers were starting again. But he ended up giving fans a final glimpse of the old Bo. Only now people were wondering whether they would see Bo on the gridiron at all in 1985.

Unlike his sophomore year when he gave up baseball for track, Bo now geared up for the 1985 baseball season. As the Auburn team began diamond play, Bo took time out to accept a Southland Olympia Award, given annually to nine young athletes by the Southland Corporation for accomplishments in the amateur sports world. He joined such former winners as Carl Lewis, Greg Louganis, Ralph Sampson, Mary Lou Retton, Mark Breland, Alberto Salazar, and Scott Hamilton.

Former Olympic decathlon champion Rafer Johnson spoke about Bo when the award was presented. "If ever an athlete exemplified the principles of the Olympia Award, that athlete is Bo Jackson," Johnson said. "He is a great athlete, a fine student, and a person eager to give of himself to others. Of the hundreds of nominations received by our committee, Bo's credentials were easily the most impressive."

Bo called the prize "the most important trophy I've ever received in a lifetime of receiving trophies." Then he added: "Receiving this award just increases my spirit to continue my education, my athletics, and the work I'm doing with children."

By that time, Bo had chosen family and child development as a major, a field of study not generally associated with All-American gridders. So his professed intention of working with children someday had to be taken seriously. Kids had always meant a lot to him, and he rarely turned down a special request to help a youngster.

One time he received a letter from a nurse in Mississippi who was treating a boy who had lost a leg three months earlier after being hit by a car. The youngster's recovery was slow and painful. He refused to eat, and his weight had dropped from 130 to 90 pounds. The nurse knew that the boy, Jon Greenwood, was a big Bo Jackson fan, and she asked the youngster if he would eat better if she got him Bo's autograph. That was her request when she wrote, even enclosing a self-addressed, stamped envelope.

Instead of a letter and autograph, Jon got a phone call. He couldn't believe he was talking to Bo Jackson. Bo then sent a package of autographed pictures, some press clippings, and an Auburn media guide to the youngster. But that wasn't all. The day before a game Bo made the two-hour drive to Oxford to visit Jon Greenwood in person.

"I knew I had to come down and give him a motivational talk, just to say life ain't over," Bo said. "Now he's doing great. He's eating and doing his therapy work. I told him he can't sit around feeling sorry for himself. He's got to do things even though he doesn't always want to do them. And I think he knows I care."

There were other instances, but one that sticks in

the mind of head trainer Herb Waldrop was the time
Bo heard about a youngster in Birmingham who had a
terminal illness. One of the boy's greatest wishes was
to meet Bo Jackson.

"Bo had already made arrangements to leave on a
hunting trip when he heard about the boy," Waldrop
recalls. "Anyone who knew Bo knew how much he
loved hunting and fishing. But when he heard the
story, he changed his plans and agreed to meet with
the youngster. That, in itself, isn't real unusual. There
are a lot of athletes who will meet with sick youngsters.

"But Bo did something extra. Not only did he meet
with the boy and try to encourage him. He also
maintained frequent contact with him right up until
the youngster passed on. And he did all that on his
own. No one had to ask him, plead with him, or
anything like that. It was just Bo."

Then, in the spring of 1985, "just Bo" began to
make big news on the baseball diamond. After skipping the sport his sophomore year, he returned with a
vengeance, using his speed and power to dazzle teammates and opponents alike. And, of course, before
long the scouts were back, swarming all over during
Tiger games.

On April 2 the Tigers ventured to Athens, Georgia,
to meet the Georgia Bulldogs. Bo grounded out his
first time at bat and received a chorus of boos from the
partisan Bulldog fans. His next time up, however, he
got even, picking out a pitch he liked and blasting it
high and deep to left center field. The ball slammed
into the lights atop a tower 85 feet above the 402-foot
mark at the fence.

As Bo circled the bases the fans couldn't believe the mammoth blast. Bob Behler, from the Georgia Sports Information Office, said the ball "was still going up or had just reached its apex when it hit the tower. Without the tower it probably would have gone 600 feet."

Bo wasn't finished yet. Before the day ended, he blasted two more home runs and a double, and the fans who had jeered him gave him a standing ovation. With a performance like that, they had no choice. It was incredible. After the Georgia contest Bo was batting .395 with 16 home runs and 41 RBIs in 39 games. He also had eight stolen bases in eight attempts. And while he might not yet have been a polished ball player, his raw talent and potential seemed limitless.

"When you talk about a player like Bo Jackson, I'm sure there aren't enough superlatives to describe his skills," said Auburn coach Hal Baird. "I've never seen a player with the combination of skills he has, and that includes my experiences in pro baseball."

Bo's rousing return to the diamond raised the questions all over again about baseball versus football. Bo gave an answer that would soon become his stock-in-trade when asked which sport he preferred.

"I like football best during the football season and baseball best during the baseball season," he said. "In other words, I enjoy both sports a lot, and I have not closed the door completely on playing pro baseball. I still have all my options open."

Up to that point it had been pretty much assumed that Bo's pro future would be on the gridiron, where it was acknowledged he would be an instant star. In baseball, he was still short on experience and actual playing time, so he was really catching up. If he turned pro, he would probably have to spend a few years in the minor leagues with no guarantee of stardom. Yet, because of the way he was playing now, it became apparent that he could become a high pick in the upcoming free agent draft. Once again speculation rose, and the question that would soon become part of his life was asked once again: What would Bo do?

When the season ended, Bo was batting .401 with 17 homers and 43 RBIs in 42 games. Baseball was suddenly in the forefront again, especially with the draft upcoming, and the superlatives regarding Bo's ability never seemed to stop.

"Bo Jackson is the greatest prospect I've seen in 35 years of scouting," said one big league scout. "I'm talking about the tools to do everything. He's good for the game, and the game would be good for him."

The easiest solution would be for Bo to try pro baseball in the summer, then return to complete his college football career in the fall. The Denver Broncos' great quarterback, John Elway, did that while still at Stanford University. He played for a Yankee farm team one summer, then decided he wouldn't have the same impact in the sport as he would on the gridiron.

The problem was that in the Southeastern Conference (SEC) the rules prohibited Bo from doing that. An athlete could not play professionally in one sport while retaining his amateur standing in another. So when the California Angels grabbed him in the twentieth round of the draft, he had to make a decision.

Scouting director Larry Himes wanted to sign Bo very badly. He projected him as a possible starter in the Angels' outfield by the end of the 1986 season or early in 1987. That would mean he'd have a relatively short time getting fine-tuned in the minors.

"Reggie Jackson spent 180 days in the minors; Kirk Gibson spent 142," Himes said. "That's about what we figure Bo would need—500 to 700 at-bats to get his rhythm and fine-tune his skills."

Himes tried two other approaches. He said the Angels were considering taking the SEC to court to challenge the rule about a player not being able to retain eligibility in one sport while playing pro in another. He also tried to convince Bo that baseball offered an opportunity for a much longer and more lucrative career.

"We've done some research on running backs in professional football, specifically backs of pro bowl stature," Himes said. "Statistics show that the length of their careers is usually about five years. On the other hand, our senior players are reaching their most productive years when they are 28. Our Reggie Jackson is 39 and making more money than any running back in the NFL."

Bo knew these things, and he also let the Angels know that challenging the SEC rule wasn't the way to go. But Larry Himes wouldn't quit. He told Bo that if he had announced he wanted baseball, he would have been the number one player chosen, and that the Angels' owner, former cowboy movie star Gene Autry, was among the most generous in the game. Bo was aware of that, also. But Himes had a now-or-never attitude.

"We know that if Bo doesn't decide to play baseball this year, that's it. He'll have the NFL draft, and being a Heisman Trophy candidate with all that hoopla, he'll probably decide to play football, which would be a mistake."

Bo, of course, weighed the pros and cons. Not wanting to keep the Angels dangling, he made his decision quickly and decisively.

"I was thrilled to have been drafted by the California Angels," he said at a press conference. "It's great to know that there's an opportunity out there for me to play baseball. But as I've told the people out there, I'm going to play football at Auburn next season, and I will not make a decision to play football or baseball professionally until after that."

That was it. Bo would be coming back to Auburn for his senior year, and baseball—if it was going to be baseball—would have to wait. He spent the summer months at Auburn, catching up on classes and getting ready for his final gridiron campaign. As soon as everyone knew he was returning, they made him the odds-on favorite to win the Heisman Trophy. It seemed that the pressure would never go away.

There was, however, a major change for the Auburn team before the season even began, one that must have been welcomed by Bo and all those who enjoyed watching him. After four seasons of running the wishbone formation, Coach Dye and his staff decided to switch to the I-formation. That formation always featured a single back—the tailback—to carry the football. Bo Jackson was the living definition of a tailback.

While Herschel Walker was setting records during his career at Georgia, he always ran from the tailback slot in the I. In three years Walker carried the football

944 times, compared to the 372 carries Bo had in three years of running the wishbone. Apparently the Tiger coaching staff realized that they had a super player and that they weren't fully utilizing his talents. In fact, during his first three years Bo had 20 or more carries on only three occasions.

Of course the Auburn coaches explained the switch to the I in terms of a total team concept, but there was little doubt that Bo was a major reason for the change. Once the change was announced, there was next to no argument about who was the odds-on favorite to win the Heisman. Bo again shied away from the media hype and said he wasn't running for the Heisman, he was running for Auburn. He often seemed shy and reluctant around members of the media. His speech impediment had improved greatly since high school days, but he still didn't like a lot of attention.

"Bo is really a special person," said Auburn's sports information director, David Housel. "Football is only a minor part of it. It's the type of person he is. He's not simple, but he's genuine. He's sincere. The great pleasure of his life is little things. He's not overly impressed by big impressive things. But the thing that really makes him unique is that everybody tries to make his life complex and he has been able to maintain simplicity."

One of the little things Bo liked was running the football. He told people that his goal was to rush for more yardage than in his previous three years combined. And that would mean more than 2,500 yards (his three-year total was 2,517 yards). It didn't seem like a realistic goal until Auburn's first game against Southwestern Louisiana. In that one, Bo Jackson was virtually unstoppable, a bolt of lightning that struck from everywhere.

Bo carried the football 23 times in his 1985 debut, gaining an amazing total of 290 yards, an average of 12.6 yards per carry. He had 10 runs for first downs, and scored touchdowns of 7, 47, 76, and 12 yards. The Tigers won easily, 49–7, and Bo's debut received headlines nationwide. There was no way he could hide now. The spotlight was all his.

By the end of the first quarter alone, Bo had 181 yards on just his first six carries. He had 206 yards by halftime and took it from there. The Tigers were ranked second nationally in the preseason polls, and as long as Bo stayed healthy, it looked as if they would be a force to be reckoned with.

"I had a feeling we would be pretty good offensively," Coach Dye said afterward. "One thing we did differently today is that we played the front line a little longer to see how long Bo could run. Now we feel if we get mistake free, we can move the ball on any team we play."

Bo wasn't the only back who had a big day. His understudy, Brent Fullwood, rambled for 173 yards on just 11 carries. With two backs gaining a total of 463 yards the Southwestern Louisiana defense obviously left something to be desired. But Bo admitted that the I-formation helped him and had definite advantages over the wishbone.

"There isn't as much blocking in the I," he said, "and the running is mostly north and south. There's not a lot of east and west running that you do in the wishbone. And I don't think I got as tired running the ball today as I did when we were in the wishbone."

By the start of his senior year at Auburn, the Bo Jackson legend was growing by leaps and bounds. He gained 290 yards in his first game as a senior. This photo of Bo leaping over a live alligator was part of a commercial shot several years later. But when he was an Auburn senior, many thought of him as Superman already. *(AP/Wide World Photo)*

When he rushed for 205 yards on 30 tries a week later against Southern Mississippi, it looked as if he was really on his way. This time his longest gain was just 34 yards, and his two scores were both from two yards out. But like all the great tailbacks before him, he pounded at the defense all afternoon, wearing them down and winding up with more than 200 yards for a second straight week. Now the superlatives really rolled in.

But in week number three against Tennessee, Bo and the Tigers both suffered a setback. Though he was not on a 200-yard pace, Bo was still gaining some solid ground against the Vols, but the Tigers were not able to sustain the attack. Late in the third quarter, Auburn trailed 24–0 as Bo got the ball on a draw play up the middle. A Tennessee defender grabbed his leg, and Bo fell on his left knee. He got up limping and walked to the sidelines.

Bo watched the rest of the game as the Vols completed a 38–20 victory over the Tigers. Bo had 80 yards on 17 carries at the time of his injury. It wasn't a 200-yard game, but it still left him as the nation's leading rusher with 575 yards in three contests. Some of the fans wondered why Bo hadn't come back in. He didn't seem to be hurt that badly.

"I looked back on last year's game with Texas," Bo said. "If I go back out there, I could get hurt worse."

The Texas game was where Bo separated his shoulder after playing with a lame ankle. This time, the injury was diagnosed as strained knee ligaments, but it wasn't serious and he was expected back the following week.

"It hurts like a toothache," Bo said during the

week, "but I don't think it will keep me out of the Mississippi game."

It didn't. Bo came back against the Rebels with a vengeance, racing to a 240-yard day and lugging the ball 38 times. Those were Herschel Walker–type stats, and something he could never have done out of the wishbone. A week later he ran 176 yards on 36 tries against Florida State, giving him 991 yards after five games and leaving him just nine yards shy of becoming only the second player in college football history to gain 1,000 yards in his first five games of the season.

A week later he did it again, this time gaining 242 yards in 32 tries against Georgia Tech. It was his fourth 200-yard game of the season, and it gave him 1,233 yards in six games, already topping his total yardage in his All-American year, 1983. With five games still remaining, a 2,500-yard season seemed somehow within his reach. He was again being compared with Herschel Walker and talked about as a potential record breaker and Heisman Trophy winner.

"I know where I am this fall as far as records are concerned," said Bo. "But I don't really think about them. All I'm thinking about is winning on Saturday. I'm running for Auburn, not the Heisman."

There was a lot to what Bo said. He was running for Auburn, all right. In fact, the Tigers were losing their game with Georgia Tech, 14–10, in the fourth quarter. Then they began driving from their own 20. Bo ran a sweep right for just four yards. On the next play he ran a draw. Only this time he broke it and broke it big, going 76 yards for his only score of the game, yet it turned out to be the game winner. Auburn had a 17–14 win, and Bo's 242 yards were a major part of the attack. There was little doubt that he was the Tigers' main man.

He proved it again against Mississippi State, gaining 169 yards on 28 tries, scoring two more touchdowns, and leading the Tigers to their sixth win against a single loss. There seemed no stopping him on his way to a consensus All-American season and probably the Heisman Trophy. In addition, he still had a shot at a slew of rushing records. But the very next week, when the Tigers met tough Florida, Bo's season would take a strange and controversial twist.

The Florida defense was always a tough nut to crack, but Bo kept pounding. Sometimes the Gators would bend, but they wouldn't break. There was just about a minute remaining in the half. Florida had a 7–3 lead, and Bo had just 48 yards on 15 carries, his lowest first-half total of the season. On his final run of the half, Bo gained just three yards on a sweep before being hit by a pair of Gator linebackers.

Suddenly he was leaving the sideline and walking with a slight limp toward the Auburn dressing room. When the team returned to the field for the second half, Bo wasn't with them. He trotted slowly back to the sideline with 13 minutes left in the third period. But he came into the game only once, in the fourth quarter, and carried a single time for no gain. Though Auburn had taken a 10–7 lead in the third, the Gators rallied to win it, 14–10.

"I caught somebody's knee between my thigh pad and my knee pad," Bo said afterward. "I got a thigh contusion that they worked on at halftime. It got to a point where it felt loose, so I went back in. Then it spasmed up again."

Then Bo added, "It's always tough when you sit on the sideline and watch your team out there playing. I wanted to go out there, but I couldn't."

That probably should have been the end of it, but it wasn't. His teammates defended him and also felt they should have won it with or without Bo.

"We know one man doesn't move our offense," said Bo's good friend, fullback Tommie Agee. "It takes all 11 players. There wasn't any mental letdown when Bo went out. If anything, it was a pickup."

But that didn't stop the whispers. Bo had now come out of two games—Tennessee and Florida—with injuries some felt were not severe enough to warrant his not trying to tough it out to help his team win. Several opposing players questioned his toughness, his courage, and his dedication, and the writers picked up on the comments.

"I was kind of disappointed he wasn't out there in the second half," said a Florida linebacker. "All week all I heard was Bo Jackson this and Bo Jackson that. It was kind of sickening. But he has a great career ahead of him. Maybe he doesn't want to take chances. If he gets slightly hurt, he takes himself out."

And an Auburn assistant coach, who remained anonymous, supposedly said to a reporter, "I don't think he would have taken himself out if he had run for 60 yards. But when he got stuffed [by the Florida defense], he was ready to come out."

Head coach Pat Dye felt compelled to come to his star's defense. Said Dye: "I don't know how badly he is hurt, but I do know you don't run for 1,400 yards in seven games without courage."

Auburn trainer Herb Waldrop thought it was ridiculous to question Bo's courage in view of the way he had handled the separated shoulder the year before.

"Bo has as much or more courage than any athlete I've ever seen," said Waldrop. "He is a world-class athlete who was willing to go out there and risk reinjuring a shoulder just to help his teammates."

It was indeed unfortunate that the injuries occurred in such a way as to make Bo look bad. Bo's high school baseball coach, Terry Brasseale, felt Bo got a bad rap because of the stoic way he often handles injuries.

"I think one reason people came down on Bo was because the camera caught him standing on the sidelines and not getting some kind of treatment," Brasseale said. "Because he wasn't doing anything just then, people assumed he wasn't hurt that badly. But what a lot of people don't know is that Bo is so muscular that his muscles can really tighten up."

After the game Bo's leg was put in an ice-water sleeve, with ice water and pressure used to stop the internal bleeding. That night he was walking with the aid of crutches.

Yet it seemed that Bo-bashing by sportswriters had suddenly become voguish. More comparisons with the SEC barometer, Herschel Walker, again surfaced. One writer from Atlanta, Georgia, used each man's games against Florida to create a comparison between the former Georgia star and Bo.

"In three games against Florida," the man wrote, "Herschel gained 649 yards. That's 216.3 yards per game, 216.3 yards against the SEC's fiercest hitters. In four games against the Gators, Bo gained 283 yards— total. Granted, he was coming off the separated shoulder last year and he hurt his thigh this time, but durability counts. Herschel took it all and didn't fall, took it every game for three years and kept barging. He was a fortress on foot, reliable and relentless, greater than the great Bo."

What was happening really wasn't fair. A few people were jumping on what they perceived as weakness, or even failure, and condemning a very great athlete. Though Bo said he had stopped reading the sports pages in high school, he nevertheless felt he had to defend himself and his team against the rising tide of criticism.

"What kind of fans criticize their teams when they lose and cheer them when they're winning?" he asked. "I don't consider them true fans. As for myself, when I feel the need to take myself out when I'm hurt, I will do that. Then I'll tell the trainer what the problem is."

That seemed closer to the truth. In fact, how could people say that Bo didn't rise to the occasion in big games when he had gained 114 yards in the pressure-packed Alabama game as a freshman? In addition, he played a number of his best games against top teams. And during his senior year he had already played with a bruised knee and back spasms.

"Jackson toughs it out and plays every Saturday," said another writer, who followed the Auburn team. "You've got to remember that every defensive player on every squad Auburn plays wants a shot at the great Bo Jackson, Heisman Trophy Candidate. It's like hunters going after big game."

The big game returned the next week against East Carolina, and it was soon obvious that Bo still wasn't 100 percent recovered. He could easily have sat out a week, but he chose to play. He gained just 73 yards on

14 carries and didn't score. It was a very un-Jackson-like performance. Some said that the Heisman Trophy, which Bo seemed to have locked up two weeks earlier, was again up for grabs. Bo's star had definitely dimmed.

The following week he began coming back. Playing a strong game against Georgia, Bo gained 121 yards on 19 carries, including a 67-yard jaunt for a touchdown. He also caught 48 yards' worth of passes as the Tigers won, 24–10. The only concession to his injury was that he alternated with Brent Fullwood at tailback for most of the game.

"I hadn't practiced or run much lately," Bo said. "I was probably only about 95 percent, but the long run gave me a chance to test my legs. It felt great to break out of there."

Heisman Trophy questions were also coming with increasing frequency, often forcing Bo to discuss something he tried to avoid.

"I haven't set a goal to win the Heisman," he said, "because if I expected it, I might go up to New York and they might give it to someone else. And I wouldn't want to live with that letdown. If I win it, great. If I don't, I won't lose any sleep. So let's say it's in the back of my mind right now and it's going to stay there. Besides, we've still got one more game to play."

And that one more game was with Alabama, the big game for the Tigers each and every season. It was the game each team wanted to win the most. Bo, of course, had been a hero against the Tide his first two years and then had run the wrong way on the potential game-winning play as a junior. Like all his teammates, he wanted to win this one very badly.

Bo had 1,644 yards going into the final game of the season. He wouldn't hit 2,000, but he was still putting together a great year. And one of his biggest boosters was none other than Alabama coach Ray Perkins. Perkins didn't pull any punches when he said, "Bo Jackson is the best running back in the world, college or pro."

So Alabama tried to defend against Bo, as it had for three previous seasons, but without much success. The Tide did a little better this time, keeping Bo from breaking into his patented long runs. He did pound into the Tide line all afternoon and scored a pair of touchdowns from seven yards and one yard out. As usual, the game was a dogfight. Auburn had a 23–22 lead in the final minutes. A last-ditch Alabama drive stalled 42 yards from the goal line. But as time expired, the Tide's Van Tiffin booted an incredible 52-yard field goal to give his team a 25–23 victory.

It was a bitter pill for the Tigers to swallow. They had played extremely well. So had Bo. He had carried the ball 31 times and gained 142 yards against a defense geared to stop him. His longest run was just 20 yards, so he was doing it the hard way. As a tribute to his fine play against the Tide during his Auburn career, a group of Alabama fans began chanting after the game: "Roll Tide! Roll Tide! Roll Tide!"

Suddenly—almost spontaneously—the chant changed, and the crowd in unison began to shout: "NO MORE BO! NO MORE BO! NO MORE BO!"

It was a fitting tribute to Bo, who had gained 630 yards on 90 carries against the Tide in four years. All four games were cliff-hangers. Bo was the hero in the first two, one of the goats in the third, and had played

71

his heart out in the final encounter. In fact, it wasn't until after the game that everyone knew just how hard Bo had played. The news surprised many and erased any doubts people might have had about Bo's courage and willingness to play while hurt.

The story broke the Wednesday after the game. Dr. Charles Veale, the Auburn team doctor, made the announcement—Bo had played the Alabama game with two broken ribs.

"The ninth rib is fractured and displaced," Dr. Veale explained. "The tenth is fractured but not displaced. Bo really wanted me to keep it quiet. He thought they wouldn't let him play, and he was afraid of the media treatment."

According to Dr. Veale, Bo had suffered the injury in the Georgia game, but didn't realize the severity of the injury at first.

"Being the type of person he is and taking as many hits as he takes, he felt it was just a bruise," trainer Herb Waldrop said. "But he aggravated it by falling on a fumble in practice the Monday before the Alabama game. He called me Tuesday morning and said the pain had kept him from sleeping. That's when we went to the doctor to have it checked."

Bo had played the game with a special pair of shoulder pads, which were longer in the back and protected the rib area somewhat. Yet the padding wasn't noticeable enough to tip the Alabama players to the problem. Dr. Veale was on the sideline during the entire game and said Bo did not complain of any pain before or after the game.

"A direct blow to the back was the only thing that really could have injured him," said Dr. Veale. "And the thick muscles Bo has in his back also provided a natural cushion against further injury."

There were even a few who intimated that the rib injury wasn't quite as severe as it was made out to be and that it was more or less a ploy to show people Bo could play while hurt and to sway the Heisman voters, since the balloting would be completed a few days after the game.

"That kind of thing is just why Bo didn't want to say anything about it," responded an angry Herb Waldrop.

As for Bo, he finally admitted that winning the Heisman was now important to him. "It would mean a great deal," Bo said. "Winning the Heisman means you're the top collegiate athlete in the nation. Take a look at past winners. Only good things have happened to them as far as endorsements and commercials."

Bo finished his senior year with 1,786 yards on 278 carries, an average of 6.4 yards a pop. He scored 17 touchdowns and had averaged 162.4 yards a game. He was also Auburn's all-time rushing leader with 4,303 yards on 650 carries, an average of 6.6 yards a try. He had scored 43 touchdowns while averaging 113.2 yards a game for his career. This included three years of the wishbone and his injury-plagued junior season. He topped such former Auburn greats as Joe Cribbs, William Andrews, and James Brooks, all of whom went on to great National Football League careers.

In December Bo was invited to New York to attend the presentation of the Heisman Trophy. Also invited were Iowa quarterback Chuck Long, Michigan State running back Lorenzo White, and Miami quarterback, Vinny Testaverde. And when the big moment

A proud and happy Bo Jackson poses with the coveted Heisman Trophy, given annually to the best college player in the land. Bo received it in December 1985, following a great all-American senior year.

(Courtesy Auburn University)

came, it was Bo Jackson who was called to the podium. He had won it!

"Those last couple of seconds, it really got hot down there," Bo said. "When I heard my name I gave a quick sigh. Otherwise, I can't describe the feeling. I don't think it's really hit me. This will probably all come down on me tomorrow."

The vote was the closest in Heisman history, with Bo just beating out Chuck Long. But the important thing was that he had won.

"Tell my offensive linemen that I love them and that this wouldn't have been possible without all of them," he said of the men in the trenches who had blocked for him. "I'm willing to share everything that comes with the Heisman with them. And I give all the credit to everybody back home, to my team and all the people who have made this possible. Let me also say that this was the first time since I've been in college that I was nervous."

There still wouldn't be much time to rest. Bo and his teammates, who had finished the regular season at 8–3, still had to play Texas A&M in the Cotton Bowl. There were also plans for Bo to play in the Japan and Senior Bowl games, and then finally he had to get ready for his last baseball season, which, naturally, brought up the big question: Would Bo play professional football or major league baseball? If he chose baseball he would become only the ninth of 51 Heisman Trophy winners not to play pro football.

"My love for both sports is equal," Bo said, answering a question that would be asked many times in the upcoming months. "I don't get any more gratification hitting a home run than scoring a touchdown. If I were to pick baseball, it wouldn't be because I could play 15 to 20 years and make a ton of money. I would do it because that's what I want to do. As long as I'm out there competing, I don't care whether it's chasing a fly ball or running from a defensive end."

In other words, he had not yet made his decision. Bo finished his football career by giving his usual outstanding performance in the postseason games, then made the immediate swing to baseball. And once he was on the diamond, his obvious talent began attracting attention once again.

"If he puts it all together he could hit 40 to 50 home runs, steal you that many bases, play center field, and run the ball down from anywhere," said one scout. "He may have the most natural talent of any prospect I've ever seen."

Bo didn't get off to a real fast start in the 1986 season. The Tigers won their first five games, but Bo didn't hit his first homer of the season until the fifth game, a 16–2 rout of Samford. After that he slowly seemed to get into a better groove. The home runs were coming, though his batting average hovered around the .250 mark. It could have been because of all the pressure.

Then, in late March, when the Auburn baseball season was in full swing, Bo took time out for a quick trip to Florida. The Tampa Bay Buccaneers had the first pick in the April National Football League draft, and they were leaning toward choosing Bo. They had asked him to come to Florida for a physical examination, not an unusual procedure for a team ready to sink big dollars into a rookie player.

The problem was that Tampa Bay paid for Bo's

Pro football or major league baseball? This was the question on everyone's mind as soon as Bo's collegiate career ended. Bo himself often joked about the decision as he thought it over and listened to offers. Sitting with his Auburn football coach, Pat Dye, Bo told reporters that he would make his choice by drawing names from a hat.
(AP/Wide World Photo)

transportation to Florida and back. By allowing the pro team to pay for his flight, Bo had violated Southeastern Conference rules. In the eyes of the SEC, he was now a professional, and the SEC had no choice but to take away his remaining college eligibility. The news was a shock to Bo, his fans, and his teammates. His college baseball season would be ending abruptly after 21 games.

"I regret very much that this has happened," Bo said. "It was an honest mistake. Had I known it would jeopardize my eligibility, I never would have gone. I was under the impression it was within the rules. I know now I should have contacted someone in authority at Auburn before I went to Tampa, but at that time I didn't realize I was doing anything against the rules."

In 21 games—he actually played in 20, suited up against Alabama, but was scratched from the lineup when the eligibility question arose—Bo had batted just .246. But he led the Tigers with seven homers and 21 runs scored. He was five for five in stolen base attempts and had 14 RBIs. It wasn't a great year, but there was still no denying his talent.

What now? Bo Jackson not playing ball is like a fish without water. Some thought he might leave Auburn immediately, and most figured it was now a certainty that he would play in the NFL. The prevailing opinion was almost totally in that direction.

"I don't think Bo is ready right now to compete in the big leagues," said his Auburn baseball coach, Hal Baird. "He could play defense and run the bases, but to handle big league pitching—he's just not ready for that."

Former major leaguer Milt Bolling, who was then a scout in the Mobile area, said he couldn't see Bo going straight to the big leagues.

"He has too many holes because he hasn't faced enough pitching," said Bolling. "Baseball is a game you've got to play often to get your timing and skills down. There's a big difference between having the ability and putting it together."

And Ben Wade, director of scouting for the Los Angeles Dodgers, also put in an emphatic vote for football. "He's got to play football," said Wade. "He's not the best [baseball] prospect in the country. The money is not even going to be close. He's got some tools, but there are a lot of kids in class-A ball with better tools than him right now."

Syd Thrift, general manager of the Pirates, the team with the first choice in the upcoming draft, all but dismissed the possibility of his team taking Bo.

"It [Bo's losing his eligibility] didn't have any effect on my plans," said Thrift. "It might have some on his."

Meanwhile, the NFL Bucs were ready to welcome Bo with open arms. The team had been running a one-back offense with the versatile James Wilder carrying most of the load. When asked what the team would do if Jackson came aboard, Coach Leeman Bennett answered without hesitating. "We would go to the two-back system if we got Bo," he said.

There didn't seem to be much doubt in which direction Bo would go. The opinions were just about unanimous. Bo would be an instant star, maybe even an All-Pro, as a rookie in the NFL. As a baseball player he would need seasoning in the minors. More than one "can't miss" prospect had withered and died on a farm team over the years, playing well in the minors but never making the transition to the bigs.

By April, with the NFL draft approaching, the wheels really began to turn. The Buccaneers had announced their intention of drafting Bo. They wanted to sign him even before the official draft, which was perfectly legal, or maybe work out a deal where they could draft him and then trade him for two or three established players and a handful of future choices. That had also been done before. Once the word was out, several NFL teams, including the San Francisco 49ers and Minnesota Vikings, contacted Tampa Bay about working out a possible deal.

"We are very serious about it and have made an offer," said 49ers general manager John McVay.

Said Vikings GM, Mike Lynn, "Bo fits into our type of offense. He catches the ball as well as any player in the league."

But Lynn added something else, something that was on everyone's mind. He said that before his club would seriously pursue Jackson, they had to be sure that Bo was committed to a pro football career.

That was still the rub. Bo wouldn't give an answer. A week before the NFL draft, he still wouldn't make a total commitment to one sport. By this time Bo had chosen the Mobile, Alabama, law firm of Miller, Hamilton, Snider, & Odom to represent him. Thomas Troy Zieman and Richard Woods were the attorneys who would do the bulk of the negotiating for Bo.

When the lawyers met with Bucs owner Hugh Culverhouse before the draft, they found he wouldn't discuss money unless Bo made it clear he was giving up baseball.

"He was basically saying," Zieman related later, "that unless Bo asked to play with them they weren't even going to make him an offer. Which is a strange way to deal with a Heisman Trophy winner."

Nevertheless, on April 29, 1986, Bo Jackson became the first player taken in the NFL draft—tabbed, as expected, by Tampa Bay. But Bo continued to play it coy—he said he wouldn't make a decision until the baseball draft, which would be held in June. Several baseball teams, including the Angels and the Toronto Blue Jays, expressed real interest in Bo. Then, about three weeks before the baseball draft, the Kansas City Royals entered the picture.

The Royals had been watching Bo all along. Their Alabama scout, Ken Gonzales, had been called to McAdory High School by Terry Brasseale and knew Bo was a prospect even then. The week before the baseball draft, Bo was in Kansas City becoming acquainted with the Royals' officials and some of the players. At that point it was generally assumed the larger initial offer would come from football. However, Bo's representatives had made it clear that baseball would have to make a substantial offer to compete with the gridiron game.

The baseball teams wanted the same thing Tampa Bay had asked for—a definite commitment that if drafted Bo would play baseball. The only thing coming out of the Jackson camp was word that Bo favored Kansas City over the Angels and the Blue Jays. Finally, on draft day, word came that the Royals had tabbed Bo on the fourth round, the 104th player chosen in June of 1986.

"Bo was on cloud nine," said Richard Woods. "Up to that point I would have bet that he would play football. Even I didn't know what he would do. I don't think he had yet made a decision, but because of how happy he was I felt there was a great likelihood he'd play baseball. He was just thrilled getting drafted by Kansas City. After all, they were the defending world champions."

Never before had two major professional sports wanted a single athlete so badly. Bo's lawyers didn't want to get into a situation where they played one team against the other, so they asked both the Buccaneers and the Royals to make their best offer and then they would decide.

Tampa Bay made their offer first, but owner Hugh Culverhouse added that if Bo didn't accept within a week it would be withdrawn. It was a questionable tactic, since the Royals were being sweet as sugar. Then they made their offer. On June 18 Bo met with his advisers and attorneys to consider both. As expected, the football offer was considerably higher in terms of immediate dollars and money over the first few years. In fact, Tampa Bay's offer was over four times what the Royals put forth.

But Bo felt that the Bucs had broken some promises and also had given him too many ultimatums, including the threat of no negotiations unless he gave up baseball. By contrast, he liked the K.C. people and despite the difference in money, the Royals' offer was the largest ever given to an untried rookie. Then the Royals sweetened the pot by a little bit more, and that was all Bo needed.

His announcement shocked the sports world. The nation's best collegiate running back decided to become a professional baseball player!

When Bo decided to play for the Kansas City Royals, his decision shocked the sports world. But Bo and his mother, Florence, were overjoyed. A big hug from Mom and a Royals' cap seem to be all Bo needed to bring out the smiles.
(AP/Wide World Photo)

PART

THREE

Not surprisingly, Bo's decision made headlines everywhere. It was hard for sports fans to believe that a guy considered a surefire superstar in the National Football League, with an earning potential in the millions, would chuck it all for baseball. After all, didn't Hall of Famer Ted Williams once say that hitting a baseball was the most difficult skill to master in all of sports? And there was still no guarantee that Bo Jackson could hit a baseball on a regular basis, especially if it curved, dipped, sailed, dropped, or knuckled.

In the early part of the century, another great football player had tried his hand at major league baseball. Jim Thorpe, the great Native American athlete, is remembered today as an all-time great on the gridiron and as a tremendous track performer as well. But as a baseball player—well, he just couldn't hit the curveball. During his six seasons in the majors, Thorpe was little more than a part-timer. He quit in 1919 to return to the gridiron full-time. His lifetime average was a weak .252 with just seven career home runs.

So Bo's surprising decision was questioned in many circles. The general consensus was that he was taking a risk. But by the same token, if his gambit failed, he could easily return to football, where his natural talents and instincts for running the football would undoubtedly return quickly.

One person who had a theory as to why Bo made the decision he did was his high school coach, Dick Atchison.

"I was his football coach and I wasn't really surprised by his decision," said Atchison. "We had a day for Bo back home early in the spring of his senior year at Auburn. Tampa Bay had already announced their intention to draft him, and Bo told me that day there was no way he was going to sign with Tampa Bay and play football at that time.

"I think it might have been different if he had been drafted by a West Coast team. Bo always loved the West Coast. While he was at Auburn he got to go out there for the Bob Hope Kodak Special and then for the *Playboy* preseason All-America team. So had it been the Rams or Raiders who picked him in '86, he might have signed. But I don't think he hit it off with Tampa Bay owner Hugh Culverhouse from the beginning. Plus the Bucs were the doormat of the NFL then. So they weren't a very attractive offer even with the money. And you've got to remember, money was never Bo's number one thing."

So the deal was done, and the many fans of Bo's

gridiron exploits had to accept the fact that they wouldn't be seeing their hero perform with the pigskin—at least not for a while. When the school year ended, he reported to the Royals shortly after signing and was assigned to the Memphis Chicks of the Southern League. It was double-A ball, the minor leagues, the starting place for most ball players. But the Royals were hoping they wouldn't have to keep one of the most famous and recognizable athletes in America down on the farm for too long.

"All along it has been the Royals' philosophy not to push players," said a Kansas City official. "We think double-A is where Bo should start. But we want to see him in the major leagues before September 1.

"Bo knows he needs some fine-tuning. He knows he needs some help. We want him in the Memphis lineup and playing as soon as possible."

Bo's professional debut was set for June 30 at Chicks Stadium in Memphis. The game was a sellout. Bo had not played competitively since he was declared ineligible at Auburn some three months earlier. A lot of people were curious about how he would fare. When he calmly stroked in an RBI single in his very first at-bat, the crowd went wild. Yet this was baseball, and not even Bo Jackson could make it a Cinderella story. Hits came hard in his first few games. He wasn't about to become an instant superstar.

On July 13 Bo belted his first professional home run, a three-run shot at Charlotte. But in his first 12 games with the Chicks, Bo was hitting just .089 with four hits in 45 trips to the plate. At that point it seemed that he might need more than a little fine-tuning. Bo himself was probably wondering if he had made the right decision when he picked baseball. But shortly after that the hits began to come. Maybe Bo Jackson was a baseball player after all.

In fact, Bo went on a pretty good tear, good enough to be named the Southern League Player of the Week from July 15 to July 21. He had 11 hits in 26 at-bats, including a double, three triples, a pair of homers, eight RBIs, and five walks. With his great speed, Bo Jackson was a sight to behold running out a triple. There weren't too many infielders who wanted to be in his path when he was under a full head of steam.

His hitting continued right to the end of the Southern League season. After his horrendous 4-for-45 start, Bo went on to hit .338 the rest of the way, collecting 47 hits in 139 trips to the plate. He had an eight-game hitting streak and hit safely 40 of his last 48 games. Overall, he batted .277 for Memphis, collecting seven homers and 25 RBIs in 53 games. His only really negative stat was his 81 strikeouts in 184 at-bats.

When the Royals called him up to the big club on September 1, he became the first player in Royals' history to go from the college campus to the big league club in the same year. The next day he got his first start, opening in right field as the Royals met the Chicago White Sox. In his first big league at-bat, he managed an infield single off veteran pitcher Steve Carlton.

Again it didn't come easy. Big league pitching is a few notches above double-A. But in just his fifth contest in the bigs, Bo became only the sixth Royals rookie to get four hits in a game. He was 4 for 5, with his first run batted in, as the Royals topped Seattle, 7–6. Then on September 14, in a game at Royals

Called up to the majors for the first time in September 1986, Bo Jackson looked very happy and comfortable in a Royals uniform. At this point, thoughts of football seemed the farthest thing from his mind. But were they?
(Courtesy Kansas City Royals)

Stadium, Bo gave the hometown fans their first glimpse of the tremendous power he was capable of generating.

Facing Seattle right-hander Mike Moore, Bo caught one and drove it high and very deep to left center field. The ball sailed high over the fence and landed halfway up the embankment beyond the fence at Royals Stadium. It was a mammoth shot, estimated to have traveled some 475 feet. As Bo circled the bases all the fans had to wonder just how much he would be able to harness his power in the near future.

Though the Royals had been World Series winners the year before, the team finished the 1986 season tied for third in their division with a 76–86 record. With no pennant race, Bo got some seasoning, playing in 25 games over the final month of the season. He batted only .207, collecting 17 hits in 82 at-bats. He had a pair of homers, nine RBIs, and three steals, and he fanned 34 times. So except for the occasional flash of power, the jury was still out. By the time the baseball season ended, the NFL was already in full swing, but Bo Jackson was headed home. For the first time since junior high school, he wouldn't be playing football in the fall.

It's hard to say how much Bo missed football that first year. He seemed more concerned with making the Royals in the spring and staying in the major leagues. He didn't want another stint in the minors. Not surprisingly, he played very well in the spring, improving in every facet of his game. His natural ability remained unlimited, and the Royals didn't want to fool around—at the end of spring training, they named Bo their starting left fielder.

This time Bo started off quickly. He smacked out 14

hits in his first 28 at-bats, including three home runs and 13 RBIs. It looked as if the Royals had a tiger by the tail. Bo was looking like a superstar already, a player who could only get better with more experience. In an April 14 game with Detroit, he hit a pair of homers, including a grand slam, and drove in a club record–tying seven runs. His performance that night also gave him 12 hits and 12 RBIs in his last four ball games.

Yet Bo Jackson still wasn't consistent. Just four days after his seven-RBI performance against Detroit, Bo tied a major league record by striking out five straight times in a nine-inning game in New York. Fans who came out to see Bo hit a tape-measure home run got a glimpse of a strikeout parade instead.

Maybe there would always be days like that. It really wouldn't matter if Bo kept up the pace he had set in April. By the end of the month he was hitting .324 and already had 15 ribbys. He had also shown himself to be an exciting outfielder and base runner. But at the end of that first month of the 1987 baseball season something else happened. The annual NFL draft was being held. And Bo, because he had not signed with Tampa Bay the year before, was eligible to be picked by another team.

It didn't seem likely. After all, Bo had spurned football once, and with the start he was having with the Royals he seemed headed for baseball stardom. That's why there was a great deal of shock and surprise when the Los Angeles Raiders announced Bo Jackson as their seventh draft pick in 1987, the 183rd player taken in the draft.

Some felt the Raiders were grasping at straws, hoping against hope that Bo might have a change of heart and decide to play football. But there were those who said that Raiders owner Al Davis wouldn't have wasted a draft choice if he hadn't known something in advance. At first Bo wouldn't talk about it. He said he was concentrating on baseball. In fact, he taped a sign to his locker designed for curious reporters. It read: "Don't be stupid and ask any football questions."

So they cooled the questions for a while, but the speculation continued. Bo was still playing good baseball for the Royals, and that took the spotlight off the draft to some extent. His average had tailed off, and he was still striking out too much, but his speed could be dazzling and his power displays awesome. He was obviously the kind of player the fans came to see. And his potential as a ball player seemed unlimited. He had that rare combination of speed and power that usually adds up to a superstar. He just had to harness it and put it all under control.

Against Texas on May 29, Bo belted a pair of homers for the second time in the season, and at Seattle on June 7, he did it again, swatting two more out of the park against the Mariners. This kind of power display excited the crowd and made many predict that a maturing Bo could easily hit 40 to 50 homers a year.

By July 12, when everyone broke for the All-Star Game, Bo's average was down to .253, but he led the Royals with 18 home runs and 45 runs batted in in 79 games. The one negative was his 112 strikeouts in 277 at-bats, putting him on a pace that could lead to more than the record 189 whiffs in a season. Still, a strong second half would also put him close to 40 homers and 100 RBIs. And since Bo was still officially considered a rookie in 1987, there were very few complaints about his production. He seemed to be progressing right on schedule, maybe even ahead of schedule.

But on July 14, the day of the All-Star Game, Bo Jackson called a news conference at Auburn to make an announcement that once again stunned the sports world. He told everyone that he had signed a contract with the Los Angeles Raiders to play pro football at the conclusion of the baseball season in October. In making the announcement, Bo said that baseball was still his number one priority and that playing football would simply be an off-season "hobby" for him.

Financially, it looked like a great deal for Bo. He would receive $2.45 million over five years to play maybe 8 or 10 games a season with the Raiders. In addition, he was given a $1 million loan. And added to his $1.066 million three-year deal with the Royals, it seemed as if Bo had really pulled a coup.

Aside from the money, however, the move raised serious questions. Could Bo physically play both sports, moving from baseball to football with only a week or two of rest? And how would playing two professional sports affect his performance? The way the deal was set up, Bo would play only about half the football schedule. It would be tough to be an All-Pro or an all-time great playing only part-time. Conversely, would the grind of the football season carry over and affect the next baseball campaign?

To their credit, the Royals gave Bo the go-ahead to try to play both sports. The only change would be a restructuring of his baseball contract, inserting an injury clause in the event Bo was seriously hurt playing football.

"I have to recognize that if a man has the talents that he has, the right way to do things is to give him that opportunity to help determine how good he is in football," said Avron Fogelman, the co-owner of the Royals.

There were those who felt that Bo signing with the Raiders was step one in a plan to eventually give up baseball, maybe even at the end of the 1987 season.

"There was no talk about Bo getting out of his contract with us," Fogelman said. "The discussion was centered on how he could do both things. I don't think Bo would have ever walked out. He is a professional, a person with a great deal of pride, and doing something like walking out on a contract is incomprehensible."

Bo appreciated the fact that the Royals didn't give him an us-or-them ultimatum. "I'm glad it never came to that," he said.

The biggest reaction came from his fellow athletes and coaches. For openers, members of the Royals were visibly and outwardly upset by Bo's decision. Obviously, most felt he couldn't concentrate on one sport while getting ready to go into another.

"I guess he got the last laugh, didn't he?" said center fielder Willie Wilson. "He got us to believe him, and now we're the fools."

Outfielder Danny Tartabull was even more blunt when he said that Bo's decision to play football "would destroy the team."

Colts running back Eric Dickerson, considered by many the best in the game, didn't think Bo would be an immediate star.

"I don't think he'll be able to do it right away," said

Dickerson. "He'll play 10 games. Maybe the last five he'll be fine. But he's never played professional football, so he doesn't understand the difference in hitting."

And former Alabama coach Ray Perkins, who was now coaching Tampa Bay, the team Bo had refused to join, said he didn't like the idea or its chances for success. Perkins, by the way, had called Bo Jackson the best back in the land, college or pro, just two short years earlier.

"I want whole players, not half players," Perkins said. "If he were here, I would be afraid that Bo's part-time status would create a prima donna atmosphere and destroy what we're trying to do. I also think Bo may be in for a rude awakening. But what really surprises me is that the Kansas City Royals are allowing him to do this."

But did the Royals really have a choice? Bo was so strong-willed that once he made up his mind, it was hard to see anything or anyone dissuading him. Several other athletes had played two sports, but none of them did it for long. They usually gave up one quite quickly. But none of those players were considered as naturally talented as Bo Jackson.

Once the excitement of Bo's decision died down, it was back to the business of baseball, and this was where the first cracks began to show. Bo began to slump terribly at the plate and missed time due to a succession of minor leg injuries. It was not a good situation. For the remainder of the season he failed to reach the heights he had been approaching in the first half. Bo Jackson was a second-half disappointment.

When the 1987 baseball season ended, Bo was

hitting just .235. He had played in only 116 games, finishing with 22 home runs and 53 RBIs. He had 10 stolen bases, but fanned 158 times. However, after he announced that he had signed with the Raiders in midseason, he hit just .193 the rest of the way, with only four homers and eight RBIs in 37 games. It was far from a dream season, but Bo didn't have time to reflect. In just two weeks he would be joining the Raiders and running with a football under his arm.

There were those who felt Bo's future was in football even before he carried a single time. There were stories that he couldn't hit the curveball, that he was going to be an all-or-nothing player who would either hit a home run or strike out. That would leave his batting average in the low .200s, making him a one-dimensional ball player.

Of course, writers and columnists were often judging from afar. They didn't really know Bo Jackson and the fires that drove him. Because he had a bad second half it was easy to blame the football diversion. But he did have some minor leg injuries and missed time, and that was enough to throw the rhythm of a raw rookie out of sync. Besides, it would probably be mental strain rather than physical fatigue that determined how well Bo would fare playing two sports.

In joining the Los Angeles Raiders, Bo was becoming part of one of football's most successful franchises. Originally housed in Oakland, the Raiders were part of the old American Football League, which had merged with the NFL in 1970. Led by maverick owner Al Davis, the Raiders had always been winners, having taken the Super Bowl three times. In fact, from 1960 through 1988 the Raiders had the best record in all of pro football. They were 258–151–11 during that time. The franchise shifted from Oakland to Los Angeles in 1982 and a year later won its third Super Bowl championship.

But in 1987 the team was somewhat in decline. They had gone from a 12–4 division championship in 1985 to 8–8 mediocrity in 1986. When Bo joined them, they seemed to be on the way to a rare losing season. In addition, the club already had an All-Pro as its primary running back. Marcus Allen was a Heisman Trophy winner out of USC in 1981. He had joined the Raiders in 1982 and had three straight 1,000-yard seasons from 1983 to 1985. Allen had gained 1,759 yards on 380 carries in 1985, so there was little doubt about his ability. That raised the question of just how Bo would fit in.

Because of a brief players' strike, the 1987 NFL season was reduced by one game to 15. After winning its first three, the team had dropped five straight. Bo missed the first eight because of baseball, then joined the team at San Diego for game nine. Coach Tom Flores spotted Bo at tailback in a 16–14 loss to the Chargers, then played him only in spots against Denver the following week. When the Raiders lost their seventh in a row, 23–17, it was time to shake things up. It was announced that Bo would be in the starting lineup the following Monday night at Seattle. What's more, the game would be on network television.

Performing on such a large stage, Bo Jackson suddenly became the best back in America again, just as he was during his Heisman Trophy–winning year at Auburn. He showed it all, the great combination of speed and power, to pound at the Seahawk defenders

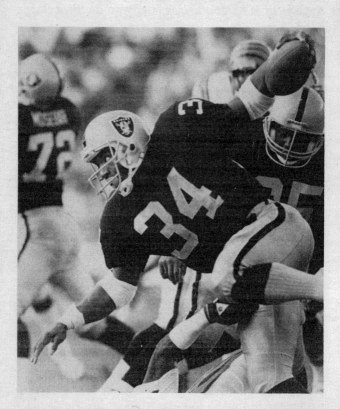

When Bo decided to play football again, in 1987, there were those who wondered if he could get back in the swing. It didn't take long. As a bruising tailback with both speed and power, Bo soon showed he was every bit as good as he had been at Auburn.
(Courtesy Los Angeles Raiders)

all game long. He slashed between the tackles, outran the linebackers and ends, and powered past the defensive backs. He was having a great game, and the Raiders were winning.

The culmination came when the Raiders had the ball at their own nine-yard line in the second half. Bo took a pitchout and ran left. Suddenly he turned on the speed and burst around the corner past the startled Seahawk defenders. Then he seemed to shift into an even higher gear, sprinting untouched 91 yards to a touchdown and a Raider record for a run from scrimmage.

But Bo wasn't finished. He continued to pick up yardage and on one of his three touchdowns he virtually ran over Seattle's highly publicized young linebacker, Brian Bosworth. To Bo, it was as if the Boz wasn't even there. When the game ended, the Raiders had a 37–14 victory and Bo Jackson had set an impressive team record.

He had run for 221 big yards, a club mark, carrying the football 18 times for an average of 12.3 yards a pop. Two of his scores came on the ground and the third when he was on the receiving end of a pass. In other words, Bo had done it all. More people began to think football was the sport for him.

Bo started the remaining four games, and while none of them was as spectacular as his Monday night debut, he certainly showed he was a back worth waiting for. He wound up with 554 yards on 81 carries, and his 6.8 per carry average was among the best in the league. He also caught 16 passes for 136 yards. In addition, he ran for four scores and caught passes for two more. As soon as the season ended, the questions began. Would Bo report to the Royals? Or would he now seek a full-time football career?

Sure enough, when spring training opened, Bo was there. And once his teammates saw he was back, they softened their attitude toward him. Some had thought he was using baseball as a wedge for a better football contract and the opportunity to play on the West Coast. But soon they began to accept him for what he was, an outstanding athlete with the physical ability to play two major sports. Now the question was, could he excel at both sports?

Before the season started, Bo instituted a new rule: he would not answer any football questions during baseball season, just as he wouldn't take baseball questions once the football season started. It was a year in which Bo-mania would really begin to heat up, for it wasn't long before the advertising world realized it had a unique commodity—an outstanding athlete who was bright and good-looking, hit home runs, and played football as a hobby. Before long, Bo's representatives would be besieged by requests to use Bo in all kinds of commercials. The following year Bo became one of the most marketable and visible athletes in America.

As to the business of baseball, however, Bo showed he was taking it seriously. He got off to another blazing start. Besides hitting well, he showed he was much improved in the outfield, in both his catching and his throwing, and he was running the bases extremely well. There was even talk about his becoming a 40-40 man—40 homers and 40 stolen bases. One thing was certain: he learned fast.

"He used to run at odd angles to the ball when he

was in the outfield," said Royals manager John Wathan. "Now he's learned how to go at the proper angles, and you can see the difference in the catches he's made."

But it was Bo's hitting that excited the fans. After a solid start in April, he really caught fire in May, showing he was an improved ball player in every phase of the game. By the time the Royals went into Cleveland for a May 31 game with the Indians, Bo seemed to be on his way to a great season. He batted .330 in 27 May games, hitting safely in 20 of them. He also had five homers and 19 runs batted in for the month, stealing nine bases along the way. For his efforts he was named Royals Player of the Month.

By May 31 Bo had a .309 batting average for the season, with nine homers, 30 RBIs, and 14 steals. The ball club had completed just 50 games, so the season wasn't yet a third gone. Bo's numbers projected over the entire year would surely announce his arrival as a star. But in that game with the Indians, everything changed.

During the game, Bo hit an infield ground ball and took off to first. Suddenly he pulled up limping and had to leave the field. The result was a torn left hamstring muscle and a trip to the disabled list. It was a tough break, especially for a normally durable athlete like Bo. But the injury had to heal, and Bo would miss 28 games in a little more than a month before his return on July 2.

The injury not only caused Bo to lose his fine edge, but also cost him a chance to be on the All-Star team. When he returned, he went into a slump. In the nearly two weeks between his return and the All-Star break, his average dropped from .309 to .287, and after the break, it dropped some more. Once again there were highs and lows. The occasional home run was offset by a brace of strikeouts. In fact, Bo tied a club record by fanning nine consecutive times in mid-September.

But while his second-half performance was again way off his first-half play, Royals manager John Wathan saw great progress in his diamond in the rough.

"Bo has made tremendous progress from last year," Wathan said. "Before he was injured in July, he was one of the best players in the league. When he came back, he just wasn't able to get it going again."

Then Wathan said what many were thinking: "Obviously, we wish Bo would play just baseball. He's proven he can do both. But for how long, we don't know."

Was Bo beginning to think about football during the second half of the baseball season? His high school coaches had said he used to get bored toward the end of one season and begin looking forward to the next sport. If he was still doing it, that kind of thinking could hurt him over a full baseball season. With football, he was playing just half a year and without the rigors of training camp. So he was more likely to stay focused.

When the season ended, Bo had become the first 25-25 player in Royals history, collecting 25 home runs to go with his 27 stolen bases. His home run total was second best on the club, and his 68 RBIs were third best among the Royals. Injuries relegated him to just 124 games, and he batted .246, gathering just 108 hits. He did cut his strikeouts from 158 to 146, but

Despite some nagging injuries that slowed him during the second half of the baseball season each year, Bo showed the kind of power at the plate that always put fans in the seats. Many of his homers were of the tape-measure variety. Look at the power in his legs and hips as he prepares to blast another one.
(Courtesy Kansas City Royals)

that was still a lot of whiffs. In view of the great start in April and May, his final numbers had to be a bit disappointing. But in addition to everything else, he did lead the Royals outfielders in assists, with 11. So he was becoming a much better all-around player. It was just that everyone expected so much because he was Bo Jackson.

It was the same when he reported to the Raiders. He came in early enough to play in 10 games, a bit more than half the schedule. If he could average 100 yards rushing for those 10 contests, he would join the coveted 1,000-yard club. Many felt he was a shoo-in.

But it turned out to be a strange, un-Bo-like season for him. Though he played in 10 games and started the final nine, he didn't seem to be quite the runner he had been in the past. He wound up with just 580 yards on 136 carries and three scores. Not only didn't he average 100 yards, he failed to gain more than 100 yards on any single occasion. His best game was an 85-yard effort on 18 carries against San Francisco. And his longest run of the year was only 25 yards, a touchdown run against Kansas City. His average per carry was only 4.3 yards, and he caught just nine passes, as opposed to 16 the year before.

Again there were some minor, maybe nagging, injuries. For instance, in a game against the New Orleans Saints, Bo gained 45 yards the first two times he carried the ball. But then he hurt a leg and had to leave the game. Though he never made excuses, he just didn't look 100 percent the entire year. Maybe playing the two sports was too much for him after all. It was something to think about, and lots of people felt that Bo was going to have to choose soon. Baseball or football? Maybe it would have to be one or the other, especially if he wanted to excel in either sport.

Then came the 1989 season, and right from the beginning there were signs that it was going to be different. For one thing, Bo was being seen more and more as a commercial spokesman. The advertising people were using his athletic versatility and his statement that football was a mere "hobby" as themes for his commercials. And Bo brought it all off. He seemed to be a natural in front of the camera, good enough for one top ad executive to say that "Bo might become the most marketable athlete in the history of the game."

Just a few months into the 1989 baseball season that same exec noted that "in just a few months he's kind of become a legend. Like Paul Bunyan. It's an amazing thing to watch."

That was because Bo was doing amazing things on the field, and each time something of an extraordinary or titanic nature occurred, the press was there to jump all over it. Just mention the name "Bo" and most people knew exactly who you were talking about. He wasn't Bill, Jack, or Joe. There were dozens of them. So even his name worked in his favor.

It started in spring training. The Royals were facing the Boston Red Sox and right-hander Dennis "Oil Can" Boyd. Bo belted one that kept rising into the clear Florida sky. After rising and rising, it not only cleared the fence but sailed over the 71-foot-high scoreboard. Experts estimated the ball traveled about 515 feet.

Early in the season the Royals were in Minnesota to face the Twins. The two teams were taking batting practice in the Metrodome. The Royals were just finishing up while many members of the Twins had already drifted onto the field to wait their turn.

"Come on, Bo. One last swing," shouted Royals hitting coach Mike Lum.

Bo jumped into the box, but instead of crossing over to the right side of the plate, the way he normally hit, he took his stance on the left side of the plate, wagging his bat toward the pitcher. He took one swing and sent a rocket over the fence, past the dome lights, and off the Hardware Hank sign on the second deck in deep right center field. The ball landed some 450 feet from home plate and fell just 30 feet short of the longest right field homer ever hit in the Metrodome. And Bo wasn't even a lefty hitter!

People couldn't believe what they had seen. Some of the players howled, others just looked. Bo walked slowly to the dugout, put his bat back on the rack, then picked up his glove. As he began walking slowly out toward left field he glanced back at Kirby Puckett, the superstar center fielder for the Twins.

"I got some work to do," he said, and Puckett just shook his head.

"Players from both teams always watch when Bo takes batting practice," said K.C. pitcher Bret Saberhagen. "There's always the feeling that you're going to see something you never saw before, and we don't want to miss it."

Scott Bradley, the Seattle catcher, said that Bo was one of only two players that fans, media people, and other ball players all wanted to see.

"Bo and [José] Canseco are the two guys that everyone wants to watch," said Bradley. "When they're done you go into the clubhouse and swap stories about the balls they hit. It doesn't matter if we haven't played the Royals for two months. Bo gets talked about. Everyone has to have a topper Bo story."

Once again Bo came out of the gate fast. Only this time it was a little faster, a little more consistent. His batting average didn't shoot up, then down. It stayed between .265 and .285, but he was hitting with power and authority. And he was attracting attention wherever he went.

"Bo is the only baseball player that you sense can do whatever he wants," said teammate Willie Wilson. "And you can't wait to see him do it."

By the end of May, Bo was the leading vote-getter in the balloting for the American League All-Star team. It was beginning to seem that everything he did attracted attention. The same night he hit his lefty homer in batting practice at the Metrodome, he belted one during the regular game, this one sailing into the upper deck in right field. It was the first time a right-handed batter had hit one there since the park opened.

Asked about it later, Bo said nonchalantly, "I hit it off the end of the bat."

In that same game Bo stole home after being caught off third on a botched hit-and-run. There was a rundown play and Bo simply took off for home. Shortstop Greg Gagne fired the ball to the catcher, but it was too late. Bo had literally outrun the ball.

"You define mistakes differently with Bo," said Manager Wathan, "because a mistake to a normal player isn't a mistake to Bo. He can outrun and outthrow mistakes. We've got some terrific players on the team this year, but it seems as if nine of ten questions are about Bo Jackson."

The Jackson mystique was growing. Bo had gotten into another habit in 1989, one born of frustration. On a number of occasions when he struck out, he would simply take his bat and break it in half over his knee. In fact, one time, he broke one over his shoulders. That may sound simple, but just try it. As Manager Wathan said, "I have to admit it was amazing to watch him take that bat and snap it over his knee like kindling."

Needless to say, that, too, made all the highlight films.

More stories. On May 11 all-time strikeout king Nolan Ryan fanned Bo four times in a Royals game against the Texas Rangers. That wasn't news. Ryan had done that to all the great hitters at some time during his long career.

"It was fun," said Ryan, reflecting the competitive spirit of great athletes. "By the last couple of times up he was on almost every pitch, so with a lead in the ninth I just reared back and threw as hard as I could. Bo was swinging as hard as he could, and I wonder what would have happened if he'd made contact."

Some twelve days later, Ryan found out. The first two times up it looked like a rerun as Bo fanned. His third time up, Ryan brushed him back with a high hard one. But Bo got right back in. The next fastball he caught, sending it into the center field bleachers at Arlington Stadium, some 461 feet from home plate. It was the longest homer at the Texas ballpark since they started measuring.

"They better get a new tape measure," said Bo.

By June Bo was still leading all the All-Star vote-getters. Then came the next step to a legend. It was simply called "The Throw."

The Royals were visiting the Seattle Mariners in a game that was tied 3–3 after nine innings. But in the bottom of the tenth Seattle made a bid to win it. Speedy Harold Reynolds was on first and took off on a hit-and-run play as Scott Bradley slammed a liner into the left field corner. As Bo ran over to field it, Reynolds was steaming toward third. And when Bo caught the carom off the left field wall, Reynolds had already cut the third base bag and was heading for home. For all intents and purposes, the game was over.

"When I saw the ball go into the corner," said Reynolds, later, "I said the game's over. It's all over."

When he caught the ball, Bo was flat-footed, with one foot still on the warning track. He was 300 feet from home plate and had no time to stride to the plate and throw. So he just fired the ball from a flat-footed stance. As Reynolds neared home plate he saw on-deck hitter Darnell Coles put his hands up as a signal to Reynolds to just come home standing.

"Suddenly, Darnell throws his hands down and I say, 'What!'" said Reynolds. "So I'm about to throw a courtesy slide and I see the ball in Bob Boone's mitt. I couldn't believe it."

Bo Jackson had thrown a 300-foot strike to home plate—flat-footed. The ball didn't even bounce, slamming into Boone's mitt on a line. Nobody was prepared for what happened. Even home plate umpire Larry Young was standing 45 feet up the third base line ready to leave the field. The first base ump had to make the out call.

"It was the greatest throw I've ever seen in my life," said Manager Wathan. "If I'm in the game another 30 years, I don't think I'll ever see another like it."

Catcher Boone, another seasoned veteran, was also shocked by The Throw. "When the ball was hit, I thought our only chance was to decoy Reynolds and hope he slowed up," Boone said. "Then I'm looking at the throw and I say, 'This ball's carrying all the way. I can't believe it.' So I forgot about the fake, caught the ball, and tagged him. Not many people in the world can throw the ball that far, and I don't know anybody who can just grab it and throw it as far and accurately as Bo did."

Reynolds, the fastest runner on the Mariners, refused to believe the throw hadn't hit the ground until he saw the tapes. And he still had to watch them several times. Bradley, who hit the ball, said, "Now I've seen it all. Is there anything this guy can't do?" And Mariner manager Jim Lefebvre simply said of Bo, "He's such a tremendous talent. God, I don't know why he even considers football."

As for Bo himself, he acted as if it were just another day at the office. Bragging and talking about himself were not his way.

"I just caught the ball off the wall, turned, and threw. End of story," he said. "It's nothing to brag about. Don't try to make a big issue of it."

But it was, because it once again showed the incredible talent that was Bo Jackson. And perhaps it was his teammate George Brett, a great player in his own right, who best summed up the things Bo was doing in 1989.

"This is not a normal guy," said Brett. "He's

superhuman. Every series, he does one thing that opens your eyes."

Finally it was All-Star Game time. Bo had stayed healthy, had kept hitting, and was the starting left fielder and top vote-getter on the American League squad. Now he was about to put on another show, this one for the National Leaguers who rarely saw him play, for the many fans and celebrities in attendance, and for a prime-time network television audience as well.

American League manager Tony LaRussa decided to put Bo in the leadoff spot. With the game at Anaheim Stadium, the A.L. was the home team and when they came up for their first at-bat, the Nationals already had a 2–0 lead. Bo stepped in to face veteran Giant right-hander Rick Reuschel.

With the muscles bulging under his tight-fitting uniform, Bo got ready. The second pitch was the one he wanted, and he took a quick, powerful swing. *Crack!* The ball jumped off his bat like a rocket, sailing high and deep to center field. The 64,036 fans in attendance all watched as the ball landed on a black tarpaulin covering an unoccupied seating area in deepest center. It was estimated that the home run traveled some 448 feet. Bo circled the bases as everyone in the park looked on in awe.

"When the ball hit the bat," said the Dodgers' Tommy Lasorda, the National League manager, "it sounded like a golf ball. I don't think I've seen anybody combine power and speed like that since Mickey Mantle."

And Manager LaRussa, who got to watch his own

José Canseco bust down fences during the regular season, said of Bo: "He's got something extra. He's in a league somewhere up in the heavens."

Bo's blast must have unnerved Reuschel, because Wade Boggs followed with another home run and the game was tied. An inning later Bo drove home the go-ahead run with a force-out. Then he showed his great speed by stealing second, jumping up, and racing to third on an overthrow by the catcher. He also got a base hit later in the game as the American League went on to a 5–3 victory. It came as no surprise when Bo was named the game's Most Valuable Player.

Once again Bo Jackson was the talk of the sports world. Seems he had a knack for doing that. He also had a knack for doing his own thing, yet few people seemed to resent him or hold a grudge against him. One of his teammates, Willie Wilson, had been upset when Bo announced he was signing with the Raiders. Yet by 1989 Wilson had done a complete about-face.

"I was upset and said some unfortunate things back then," Wilson admitted. "But as I've come to learn, Bo's such a good guy, I just admire him."

At the All-Star break, Bo had played in 81 games, more than any other Royal. He was batting .263 with 21 homers and 59 RBIs. He also had 23 stolen bases. Projected over the second half of the season, he was on a 40-40 pace in homers and steals, and seemed to be headed well over the 100 RBI mark. The Royals were chasing the Oakland A's and trying to make a race out of it. With Bo finally playing like a superstar, it looked as if the Royals had a chance.

But the second half of the season proceeded in a somewhat familiar manner. Bo began missing some

With his flair for the dramatic, Bo watches another tape-measure home run sail into the distant seats. This one came before a national television audience during the first inning of the 1989 All-Star Game at Anaheim Stadium. Bo put on a dazzling show and was named the game's most valuable player.
(AP/Wide World Photo)

games, mainly to minor leg injuries, and once again his performance suffered. This time it wasn't so much his batting average as his power numbers. He didn't exactly go into a tailspin—it was just the result of missing games and not being 100 percent.

He was hitting .263 at the break, then batted .246 in the second half to finish at .256. But after playing in 81 games the first half, he finished with 135, meaning he missed 27 contests. He wound up with 32 homers and 105 RBIs, by far his best season, but he had just 11 round-trippers and 46 ribbys after the break. The big tip-off was in his steals. Bo swiped just three sacks in the second half of the year, finishing with 26.

Unfortunately he was still a free swinger, fanning a career-high 172 times in 1989. But there was no denying that he was a baseball player, not just a football player who had gotten his priorities fouled up. The problem was he still hadn't played consistently for an entire season. The second half always saw him tail off and miss games, and his numbers dropped. Maybe it was the injuries, or maybe it was something else. Terry Brasseale, Bo's high school baseball coach, offered a theory.

"I've said this all along," explained Brasseale, "but I really think Bo gets bored with one sport. He's always had to play a bunch of different sports, and that's why I think his numbers tail off at the end of the baseball season. He's just tired of that one sport and is ready to do something else."

Dick Atchison, his high school football coach, more or less agreed, saying that even in high school "Bo used to get bored to death. He cannot just stay with any one thing. If he had to play only baseball 12 months a year, I think he'd get out of it. In fact, I think he would go crazy."

Yet the more Bo played, the more he amazed people with his athletic feats, the more he was seen in successful commercials, and the more people realized what a complex man he was. Despite his increasing visibility, which lasted nearly 12 months of the year, he was still a very private person. He had gotten married, and his wife, Linda, was a Ph.D. candidate in psychology. Bo talked about returning to school to complete the few remaining credits he needed to get his degree. And he still talked about working with children. His special affinity for youngsters was always in evidence.

"Bo is one of the few players I've ever seen who tips each individual clubhouse kid," said Boston's clubhouse manager, Don Fitzpatrick. "Not only that, but he talks to each of them about staying in school, staying away from drugs, trying to do something for society. There's really no doubt in my mind that Bo is a special guy."

But that special guy really didn't have too much free time. Completing his best-ever baseball season, he had to get ready to rejoin the Raiders. Bo didn't seem to object to a schedule that would have drained the energy from most men.

"Idle time is something that doesn't fit into my agenda" was the way he put it. "In fact, I've gotten to the point where I'm finding it hard to handle the idle time I do have."

Bo had no immediate plans to choose one sport over the other—something most other people felt he would have to do sooner or later.

"I don't feel any pressure about that," Bo said. "I am my own person and I'm happy with what I'm doing. So I don't have to make a decision whether I'm going to play this sport or the other. I'm doing what I want to do."

In a way, it was the Raiders who were getting shortchanged. They had Bo for only about 10 games of the season while the Royals had him all year. But his talent was such that Al Davis and the Raider coaches seemed to accept it. They were just glad to have him.

"Al Davis has said many times that he views Bo as a player coming off injured reserve in the middle of the season," said Bo's attorney, Richard Woods. "And Bo enjoys the busy schedule. He doesn't do it because he needs the money. He does it because he wants to."

Bo reported to the Raiders just four days before the team's sixth game of the season. That meant he would be available for 11 contests. The Raiders were 2–3 and struggling when Bo joined them. People wondered if he could be ready with just four days of practice when most players needed two months of training camp and several preseason games. But sure enough, that Sunday against Kansas City, Bo was ready to go and saw considerable action. In fact, his play had a lot to do with the outcome.

He carried the ball 11 times and gained 85 yards, 75 of them in the second half when he started getting into the rhythm of the game. Early in the fourth period he broke one for 45 yards, setting up the touchdown that gave the Raiders a 20–7 lead. They won the game, 20–14, and many thought Bo made the difference.

"I almost asked for his autograph," said Raider tackle Bob Golic. "It was exciting."

All-Pro defensive lineman Howie Long also marveled at Bo's performance. "Once he hits fifth gear, it's adios. He's like a Porsche 928."

There was simply no denying Bo's unique talents any longer. To join a football team, learn the system and plays, and gain 85 yards just five days later is nothing short of an incredible athletic feat. A week later the team lost to the Philadelphia Eagles, 10–7, but Bo was again the leading rusher with 79 yards on 20 tries. The Raider offense wasn't real strong in 1989, the passing game was not what it used to be, and even the presence of Bo Jackson couldn't guarantee a lot of points on the board. But he helped. In fact, against the Redskins the following week he did more than that.

Playing at home, the Raiders topped the Skins in a wide-open affair, winning 37–24 as Bo led all rushers with 144 yards on 19 carries. His 73-yard touchdown run in the third period not only electrified the crowd but really put the game on ice. Once again he showed his great combination of speed and power, doing the job inside as well as outside. After three games he had run for 308 yards on 50 carries, an average of 6.2 yards a pop. In fact, his per-carry average was already the best in the AFC.

A week later he was at it again. This time he ran for 159 yards on just 13 carries in a 28–7 win over Cincinnati. In that one Bo broke loose for a 92-yard touchdown run, making him the only player in NFL history to have run for two touchdowns from more than 90 yards out. He also scored the first Raider TD and helped his team control the football all afternoon. His big day also moved him into sixth place among AFC runners with 467 yards. His per-carry average

Playing for the Raiders in 1989, Bo was outstanding. Here he clutches the ball with both hands while ripping past a defender. In '89, he had a 92-yard touchdown run and 950 yards rushing to add to his résumé.
(Courtesy Los Angeles Raiders)

was up to 7.4, best in the entire league. And he was doing it after having missed the first five games of the season.

Just as in the 1989 baseball season, Bo Jackson was opening people's eyes. As a baseball player he had approached superstar status in 1989, and as a running back he was now just about there. The funny part was that during baseball season some observers were convinced he should quit football. And during football season those same people felt that if he gave up baseball, he could easily become one of the great running backs of all time.

This speculation must have amused Bo, who had said all along that he could do it. It was other people who said he couldn't. In fact, Bo was playing for his third coach in three years. Longtime Raider mentor Tom Flores had retired after Bo's rookie year, 1987. Mike Shanahan took over in 1988, and in 1989 former Raider All-Pro tackle Art Shell became the head man. According to running backs' coach Joe Scannella, these changes hampered Bo's progress.

"The first two years he had to learn two entirely different systems," Scannella said. "Now he comes in and knows the basic system, so he has to make fewer adjustments and can free-wheel a little better."

Bo got 103 tough yards on 21 carries as the team was upset by San Diego, 14–12, then ran for only 54 yards on 11 tries in a 23–7 loss to Houston. The Raiders trailed from the start in that one and had to play catch-up. Bo had to leave the game in the third quarter when his left quadriceps muscle tightened up. The same muscle was strained during the second half of the baseball season.

He had just 64 yards on 20 carries in a win over New England. Then in another victory over tough Denver, Bo had just 44 yards on 14 tries. It was obvious the leg was slowing him down. His per carry average was down to a season low, 5.7 yards a try. With just three games left, Bo had 732 yards, so he would have to pick up the pace to reach 1,000. The Raiders were at 7–6, trailing Denver in the AFC West, but they still had a shot at the playoffs as a wild card team.

Bo's injury was now being called a bruised knee. He had averaged 6.8 yards a carry in his first five games with the club, then in the next three games dropped to 3.6 yards a try. As in baseball, the nagging injuries slowed him up. Coach Art Shell said that people always expected more because he was Bo.

"Everyone thinks he is Superman," Shell said. "He never said it and I never said it. Bo's a human being just like everybody else, not some Robo football player, and he gets nicked like everybody else."

Bo bounced back against the Cardinals, getting 114 yards on 22 tough carries as the team won an important game 16–14. But the team had a major setback the next week, losing 23–17 to Seattle. Bo had 69 yards in that one, and there was some controversy surrounding him that week as well.

For one thing, the Raiders had said that Bo would still be their main man carrying the ball, even though longtime star Marcus Allen had returned from an injury. Then a reporter on one of the NFL network pregame shows said a source had told him that Bo would be giving up football for baseball after the season. Coach Shell was visibly annoyed.

"I don't have time to worry about Bo quitting football," he snapped. "I've got to worry about this football team winning games. And I haven't gotten any indication that Bo will do that. In fact, I don't know whether Bo's given that kind of indication to anybody."

Bo hadn't. Even if he thought about it, there was no way he would put it on record while his team was struggling to make the playoffs. The struggle ended a week later when the club lost to the Giants, 34–17, to finish at 8–8 and out of the playoffs. Bo had just 34 yards against the tough Giants defense, finishing the year with 950 yards on 173 carries for a 5.5 average. It had been his best season so far, but as in baseball, his pace had slowed in the later stages.

There was no doubt about Bo's ability. He had All-Star talent in both baseball and football, but people—especially sportswriters—had a hard time accepting the fact that this man could play two sports. When they saw his numbers fall off during the second half of the baseball or football season, they had a tendency to blame the other sport, the one he was not playing at the time. More and more people began to feel that Bo would have to make a choice. Early in his career, everyone thought it would be football. But as the years pass, it seems to be swinging toward baseball. And all the talk sometimes irritates Bo Jackson.

"The thing that gets my goat," Bo said, "is that you go out there and have a good game and everybody says this guy is going to be the greatest athlete. He's going to do this and do that. But go out the very next week and have a terrible game, and the stories are all turned around.

"I just want people to let me do what I'm doing. Don't try to sum up my career in one or two seasons. Let me finish it first. I don't look down the road at choosing one sport and trying to be great. I think there have been enough great athletes. I just want to be an athlete, an athlete who is also a fine person."

With a multitude of commercial opportunities sitting before him, Bo once again surprised people after the 1989 football season ended. He didn't go on a vacation; he didn't go on the banquet circuit; he didn't go to shoot a dozen commercials. Instead, he returned to Auburn University to work on his degree.

"I've never been a quitter," he said. "I put this off for three and a half years, and I thought it was due time to come back and at least get closer to getting my degree."

Bo was about five classes short of graduating, his major still family and child development. As one of his projects he was to produce an 8- to 10-minute video showing what it was like to be a student in Auburn's School of Human Sciences. Bo said part of the reason for doing the tape was "to show kids that sports and party life are not the only thing you go to college for."

He also said he wanted young people to look at him as a role model, because aside from playing sports, "I don't think there's anything I'd rather be doing than working with kids."

Bo's fellow students were very impressed by having a celebrity in their midst who didn't act any differently from them.

"I think what he's doing is a great idea," said Jennifer Goldstein, a senior who was also majoring in

Never one to do the expected, Bo again surprised people in January 1990 when he announced he was returning to Auburn to work on the few credits he needed for his degree in family and child development. Here other Auburn students stare at the celebrity in their midst as Bo walks with his internship advisor, Paulette Hill (right).
(AP/Wide World Photo)

family and child development. "It's so admirable for people to look at him and see what he's doing. I think he's putting in a pretty good word for education."

Actually he was giving up something. His attorney, Richard Woods, said that Bo's return to school "might be the most expensive quarter for any student in history. He's turning down offers in the high six figures so he can do this."

When someone remarked that most people wouldn't do this, Bo was quick to answer. "But I'm not most people," he said.

That was for sure. When March rolled around he was back in the Royals camp amid more speculation that he would soon have to choose one sport over the other. There were also new "Bo" commercials appearing. The theme was almost always Bo's athletic versatility, showing that he could do anything. The phrase "Bo knows," which was in many of his commercials, became a kind of byword for him. His visibility was higher than ever.

The 1990 baseball season was a strange one for Bo. Instead of his usual quick start, he got off very slowly. In fact, the entire Kansas City team was slumping. The Royals had gone into the free agent market over the winter and signed top reliever Mark Davis and starter Storm Davis with the hope of overtaking the defending champion Oakland A's. But injuries and off seasons for key players upset the applecart and the team floundered.

Bo also continued to struggle. For the first time in his career there were some trade rumors in the air, rumors that the Royals were willing to part with their superstar performer. Dick Atchison, Bo's high school football coach, said that the trade talk was depressing for Bo.

"It really got him down," said Atchison. "Bo isn't one of these guys who's always looking for greener pastures. He went to Kansas City and that's where he wants to stay."

But then, toward midseason, Bo suddenly snapped out of it. He began to hit home runs, drive home teammates, and play brilliantly in the outfield. He was playing center field in 1990, a position that utilized his great speed and throwing arm. He soon began adding to his array of great catches. In one game he raced toward the left center field wall, his great speed enabling him to catch up with a ball that had "double" or "triple" written all over it.

At the last second Bo reached across his body and backhanded the baseball. It was a fine enough catch as it was, but Bo had a knack for doing the unusual and unexpected. Most outfielders, making a running catch near the wall, would simply have braced themselves as they hit the wall, making sure they weren't injured while holding on to the ball. But Bo didn't bother doing that.

He simply ran up the wall, his body almost perpendicular to the ground. Then he took two more steps and hopped off. He did it with a casual ease that made it look routine. But most people watching had to wait for the replay. It was as if Bo was defying gravity, walking sideways on a wall. Once again he had made the amazing look easy.

Bo's tear continued into the All-Star break. Then on July 17, Bo and his Kansas City teammates rolled into historic Yankee Stadium to face the erstwhile Bronx

Bombers. The game almost proved to be a microcosm of Bo's baseball career.

In the first inning, Bo came up against Yankee right-hander Andy Hawkins with one man on base. He worked the count to 2–2, then went after a fastball and drove it to deep center field. Rookie Deion Sanders, who was attempting to duplicate Bo's feat of playing two major sports, went back to the 408-foot mark and watched the ball sail over his head for a home run.

Then in the third inning, Bo came up again, this time with George Brett on first. Hawkins threw, and Bo hit a rocket to deep right center. The only question about this one was where it would land. The answer was the right center field bleachers, some 464 feet from home plate, the longest blast at Yankee Stadium all year. By now the partisan New York crowd was on its feet and cheering.

He came up again in the fifth with runners on second and third with one out. At first it looked as if the Yanks would walk him intentionally. But they opted to pitch to him, and on the 1–0 delivery he reached for a low outside fastball and poked it into the right field stands for his third home run of the night. The three blasts had produced seven RBIs, and the crowd, knowing Bo would have a couple of chances to tie the major league record of four home runs in a game, began chanting, "Bo! Bo! Bo!" They knew they were watching a special athlete in action.

But Bo would never get a chance for the fourth circuit. In the sixth inning, Deion Sanders hit a liner to right center. Bo raced into the gap and threw his body into the air in an attempt to make a diving catch.

This time he didn't pull off a miracle. He missed the ball and landed hard on his left shoulder. To the dismay of the fans, he had to leave the ball game.

The diagnosis was a partial dislocation of the left shoulder. Doctors said at first the injury wasn't serious. But it turned out to be bad enough to put Bo on the disabled list for nearly six weeks. At the time of the injury, Bo had his average at a solid .270, had belted 19 home runs and driven in 57 runs. He had played in 79 games, nearly half a season. Plus he had been hot as a pistol for the month preceding the injury. So it was pretty safe to assume he was headed for his greatest season.

Unfortunately, the injury created a carbon copy of his bad luck in the second half of the past three seasons. Yet once again his tremendous potential was not realized over the full campaign. He finally returned against Seattle on August 26. Naturally, with Bo's flair for the dramatic, he returned with a bang. In his first at-bat against Mariner lefty Randy Johnson, he belted out a 450-foot home run. Bo was back.

The homer also enabled him to tie a record, since he had homered in his first three at-bats against the Yankees before his injury. So he equaled the mark for most home runs in consecutive at-bats in two games. In fact he had three hits in his return and went on to finish the season in strong fashion.

When the season ended, he had played in only 111 games, missing 51 due to injuries. But he wound up with a career-best .272 average, with 28 homers and 78 RBIs in 405 at-bats. He also had a career-low 128 strikeouts. So there was little doubt that he really would have posted superstar mumbers had he not been hurt. Of course, the critics will come out and say he's doing too much. But the way Bo plays, going all out and often putting his body on the line, can lead to injuries. As his coach with the Raiders, Art Shell, had said, Bo isn't Superman.

What he is, however, is an incredible athlete, a man doing something no one has done as successfully before him—playing America's two most popular sports, covering 10 months of the year, and playing both at an All-Star level. Will he have to choose one sport over the other someday? The consensus is yes. But those same people were willing to bet the farm that Bo was going to choose football when he came out of Auburn in 1986. He fooled them then, and he's been fooling them ever since.

Dick Atchison is among those who feel Bo will eventually choose to play one sport full-time, giving up the other.

"At the beginning of the 1990 football season, Bo will have two years left on his Raiders' contract," Atchison said. "I'm sure he'll honor that. After all, it's a good situation, but I don't know how long he can do it. I really think when the time comes to give something up, it will be football that goes."

But then Atchison said something that really sums up Bo's career so far and could very well govern it right to the end.

"You got to remember one thing," he said. "He's Bo, and people can advise him, write about him, make all the suggestions and predictions they want. But he's not gonna listen to any of them. In the end, he's gonna do what he's always done, and that's exactly what Bo wants."

Since he was a young boy, Bo Jackson has never stopped to rest.
The question now is what does the future hold? Will he continue to
play both baseball and football, or will he soon give one up. As
long as he's having fun, hitting homers and scoring touchdowns,
Bo will continue to be Bo. And only he knows what will happen
next.
(Courtesy Los Angeles Raiders)

BO JACKSON, COLLEGE STATS

Football, Auburn University

Rushing

Year	Games	Attempts	Yards	Average	TDs	Longest Gain
1982	11	127	829	6.5	9	53
1983	11	158	1,213	7.7	12	80
1984	6	87	475	5.5	5	53
1985	11	278	1,786	6.4	17	76
Totals	39	650	4,303	6.6	43	

Receiving

Year	Caught	Yards	Average	TDs	Longest Pass
1982	5	64	12.8	0	43
1983	13	73	5.6	2	44
1984	4	62	15.5	0	21
1985	4	73	18.3	0	29
Totals	26	272	10.5	2	

Baseball, Auburn University

Year	Games	AB	R	H	Average	HR	RBI
1983	26	68	14	19	.279	4	13
1985	42	147	55	59	.401	17	43
1986	21	69	21	17	.246	7	14
Totals	89	284	90	95	.335	28	70

BO JACKSON, PRO STATS

Baseball, Kansas City Royals

Year	Games	AB	R	H	HR	RBI	Avg	BB	SO	SB
1986	25	82	9	17	2	9	.207	7	34	3
1987	116	396	46	93	22	53	.235	30	158	10
1988	124	439	63	108	25	68	.246	25	146	27
1989	135	515	86	132	32	105	.256	39	172	26
1990	111	405	74	110	28	78	.272	40	128	15
Totals	511	1,837	278	460	109	313	.250	141	638	81

Football, Los Angeles Raiders

Rushing

Year	Games	Attempts	Yards	Average	TDs	Longest Gain
1987	7	81	554	6.8	4	91
1988	10	136	580	4.3	3	25
1989	11	173	950	5.5	4	92
Totals	28	390	2,084	5.3	11	

Receiving

Year	Games	Caught	Yards	Average	TDs	Longest Pass
1987	7	16	136	8.5	2	23
1988	10	9	79	8.7	0	27
1989	11	9	69	7.7	0	20
Totals	28	34	284	8.1	2	

"There is only one reason why I should ever go away."

"What is . . . that?"

He felt her body tense beneath his hands as he answered:

"If you should cease to love me."

"I shall never do that . . . you know I could never stop loving you . . . I love you with all of me . . . with my mind, my heart, and my soul."

His lips touched hers as he said:

"You have forgotten something."

"What have I forgotten?"

"Your body—your beautiful, exciting body, my darling. I want that, too."

"It is yours! You know it is . . . yours!"

"My sweet—my wild, unwilling little wife, how can I tell you how much you mean to me?"

"Not unwilling. Never . . . never again will I ever be . . . unwilling to do . . . anything you want or ask of me."

His mouth came down on hers, stifling the last words, kissing her until it was impossible to think of anything but him.

Once again she felt the flame rising within her, leaping unrestrained and wilder than it had been before.

She wanted him closer and still closer to her and she knew that the ecstasy and rapture which made her feel that he swept her towards the stars was what he was feeling too.

Then his heart was beating on hers, and his lips were demanding that she surrender herself completely and absolutely to his need of her.

"I love you!" she wanted to say, and knew that the fire that consumed them both was the true eternal love which would never die.

*   *   *

Beneath the bed a blissfully happy Bobo, having torn into pieces an expensive nightgown, a pair of trousers, and a shirt, was stalking a new prey.

He pounced on it and held it down with both his front paws in case it should escape.

A black velvet shoe embroidered with a coronet in gold thread was the best kill he had ever made.

ABOUT THE EDITOR

BARBARA CARTLAND, the world's most famous romantic novelist, who is also an historian, playwright, lecturer, political speaker and television personality, has now written over 200 books. She has also had many historical works published and has written four autobiographies as well as the biographies of her mother and that of her brother Ronald Cartland, who was the first Member of Parliament to be killed in the last war. This book has a preface by Sir Winston Churchill. Barbara Cartland has sold 80 million books over the world, more than half of these in the U.S.A. She broke the world record in 1975 by writing twenty books in a year, and her own record in 1976 with twenty-one. In private life, Barbara Cartland, who is a Dame of the Order of St. John of Jerusalem, has fought for better conditions and salaries for Midwives and Nurses. As President of the Royal College of Midwives (Hertfordshire Branch), she has been invested with the first Badge of Office ever given in Great Britain, which was subscribed to by the Midwives themselves. She has also championed the cause for old people and founded the first Romany Gypsy Camp in the world. Barbara Cartland is deeply interested in Vitamin Therapy and is President of the British National Association for Health.

Barbara Cartland's Library of Love

The World's Great Stories of Romance Specially Abridged by Barbara Cartland For Today's Readers.

☐ 11487	THE SEQUENCE by Elinor Glyn	$1.50
☐ 11468	THE BROAD HIGHWAY by Jeffrey Farnol	$1.50
☐ 10927	THE WAY OF AN EAGLE by Ethel M. Dell	$1.50
☐ 10926	THE REASON WHY by Elinor Glyn	$1.50
☐ 10925	THE HUNDREDTH CHANCE by Ethel M. Dell	$1.50
☐ 10527	THE KNAVE OF DIAMONDS by Ethel M. Dell	$1.50
☐ 10506	A SAFETY MATCH by Ian Hay	$1.50
☐ 10498	HIS HOUR by Elinor Glyn	$1.50
☐ 11465	GREATHEART by Ethel M. Dell	$1.50
☐ 11048	THE VICISSITUDES OF EVANGELINE by Elinor Glyn	$1.50
☐ 11369	THE BARS OF IRON by Ethel M. Dell	$1.50
☐ 11370	MAN AND MAID by Elinor Glyn	$1.50
☐ 11391	THE SONS OF THE SHEIK by E. M. Hull	$1.50
☐ 11376	SIX DAYS by Elinor Glyn	$1.50
☐ 11466	RAINBOW IN THE SPRAY by Pamela Wayne	$1.50
☐ 11467	THE GREAT MOMENT by Elinor Glyn	$1.50
☐ 11560	CHARLES REX by Ethel M. Dell	$1.50
☐ 11816	THE PRICE OF THINGS by Elinor Glyn	$1.50

Buy them at your local bookstore or use this handy coupon:

Bantam Books, Inc., Dept. BC, 414 East Golf Road, Des Plaines, Ill. 60016

Please send me the books I have checked above. I am enclosing $_____ (please add 50¢ to cover postage and handling). Send check or money order—no cash or C.O.D.'s please.

Mr/Mrs/Miss_____

Address_____

City_____State/Zip_____

BC—6/78

Please allow four weeks for delivery. This offer expires 12/78.